THE TRUTH OF
THE MATTER

THE TRUTH
OF THE MATTER

THE
HOMELANDERS

BOOK THREE

by
ANDREW KLAVAN

THOMAS NELSON
Since 1798

NASHVILLE DALLAS MEXICO CITY RIO DE JANEIRO

Published in Nashville, Tennessee, by Thomas Nelson. Thomas Nelson is a registered trademark of Thomas Nelson, Inc.

Thomas Nelson, Inc., books may be purchased in bulk for educational, business, fundraising, or sales promotional use. For information, please e-mail SpecialMarkets@ ThomasNelson.com.

Publisher's Note: This novel is a work of fiction. Names, characters, places, and incidents are either products of the author's imagination or used fictitiously. All characters are fictional, and any similarity to people living or dead is purely coincidental.

Unless otherwise noted, Scripture quotations are taken from KING JAMES VERSION.

Library of Congress Cataloging-in-Publication Data

Klavan, Andrew.
  The truth of the matter / Andrew Klavan.
     p. cm. — (Homelanders ; [bk.] #3)
  Summary: When eighteen-year-old Charlie West finds the one person who knows what happened to him a year earlier, he finds that remembering is painful as well as dangerous, and figuring out what to do with the new knowledge may be his toughest challenge yet.
  ISBN 978-1-59554-714-9 (hardcover)
  [1. Fugitives from justice—Fiction. 2. Amnesia—Fiction. 3. Terrorism—Fiction.
4. Adventure and adventurers—Fiction.] I. Title.
  PZ7.K67823Tr 2010
  [Fic]—dc22   2010009349

Printed in the United States of America

10 11 12 13 QG 6 5 4 3 2 1

THIS BOOK IS FOR
PATRICK HUDNUT

PART I

PART I

CHAPTER ONE

Waterman

The revolving door went around and suddenly there he was: Waterman. The one man who might know the answers; the one man who might clear my name. He stepped out of the black office tower. He stood for a moment in the gray light of the late autumn afternoon, buttoning his overcoat and eyeing the flurries of snow falling from the slate-colored sky. Then he moved off along the sidewalk, joining the crowds of city commuters and Christmas shoppers.

I followed him.

I had been sitting at the window counter in the Starbucks across the street. Nursing a strawberry-banana smoothie, watching Waterman's building, waiting. Now, I drained my cup with a rattling pull at the straw and stood up. Quickly, I zipped up my black fleece against the cold and hurried outside. As Waterman moved away, I crossed the street and joined the crowd moving along behind him.

For the first time since this nightmare began, I felt a small, dizzying thrill of hope, real hope that I might find my life again, find my way home again. Waterman was the only person I knew of who might be able to explain how a year of that life had vanished from my memory, how I'd gone to sleep one night in my own bed and woken up entangled with the terrorist Homelanders and wanted by the police for the murder of my best friend.

I shouldered my way through the dense crowds, hanging back about half a block behind my man. Waterman was a tall guy, bald except for a fringe of silver hair. His bare head rose above the other people on the sidewalk. It was easy to keep him in sight as he hurried along.

But even as my heart lifted in hope, it was racing in fear.

New York City was like some kind of paranoid

nightmare. Okay, probably not for everyone—but definitely for me. The skyscrapers and office buildings rocketing up out of the ground hemmed me in on all sides. They seemed to blot out the sky, leaving only a small strip of iron gray visible between the building tops above. Below, the avenue ran under the rising walls like a narrow canyon between towers of colorless stone. The people and cars pushing through that canyon were crushed together shoulder to shoulder, fender to fender, as if they were in some kind of steel-and-glass stampede. Horns were honking constantly. Sirens sounded every few minutes. Jackhammers stuttered loudly where workmen dug holes in the pavement. The noise was overwhelming.

And everywhere—everywhere—there were faces and eyes. The faces and eyes of ordinary citizens on their way home from work or shopping. The faces and eyes of slinking, sullen, suspicious men who might be my enemies or just city thugs. The faces and eyes of policemen—policemen and more policemen—so many—standing on every corner, sitting in patrol cars parked at the curb, studying the crowds, watchful, alert.

To someone else, maybe to anyone else, it might have all seemed exciting and dazzling and full of energy. But I knew that at any moment, any one of these thousand faces, any pair of those eyes, might turn toward me, might recognize me. At any moment, someone could point a finger and shout, "Look! That's Charlie West! Get him!"

Up ahead, Waterman turned the corner and vanished from my sight. Afraid of losing him, I pushed through the people around me more quickly, slipping between bodies padded with heavy overcoats and down jackets, brushing by briefcases and purses and shopping bags filled with wrapped boxes. I got to the corner and scanned the scene. There were fewer people on the side street and it was easy to spot Waterman as he hurried along.

I hurried along behind him. One block, then another. As we moved farther and farther from the center of town, the crowds and traffic thinned. There were fewer and fewer people on the street, fewer cars. It became harder—then just about impossible—to hide myself in the crowd. I could only hope that Waterman wouldn't turn around and see me. Even though I thought he held the secret to my missing year, I didn't know if he was a friend or an enemy. I was afraid if I confronted him on the street, he would run away—or attack me or turn me in. I just didn't know. I wanted to follow him for a while and see if I could find out more about him before I approached. I wanted to choose the time and place we met.

It was late November, almost Thanksgiving. The stores were decked with Christmas decorations. There were elaborate displays in some of the windows. I hurried past a Victorian scene with miniature electronic skaters moving over a frozen lake, past a depiction of "The Night Before Christmas" with Santa's sleigh landing on a rooftop. My eyes strayed over the animated figurines. For the first time, I dared to think that maybe I could be home for the holidays, back with my mother and father, back with my girlfriend Beth for our first Christmas together . . . or anyway, the first Christmas together that I could actually remember.

I guess my mind sort of drifted as I was thinking about that, daydreaming about it. Because all at once, I came back to the present, I looked ahead of me—and Waterman was gone.

I stopped dead. Desperately, I looked left and right. I was on a street of brownstones, quaint four-story apartment buildings pressed together in a long row, each with a stone stairway leading up to the front door. I scanned the stairways to see if Waterman was going up one of them. I scanned the doors to see if Waterman was going inside. He was nowhere.

I started walking again, started walking faster, nearly

running—rushing to get to the last place I'd seen him. I reached the spot on the sidewalk where he'd vanished.

That's when I saw the alley.

It was a passage of concrete between two brick walls. It ended in a windowless wall of stone. The passage was too narrow for a car. There was nothing in it but a pair of trash cans.

And Waterman. He was there too.

He was standing very still near the alley's end, his hands in his overcoat pocket. He was waiting there.

He was waiting for me.

I stared at him. I swallowed hard. I guess he'd known I was behind him all along. I guess *he* was the one who had chosen the place for us to meet.

Well, there was nothing much I could do about it now. I could either speak to him or walk away. And after all this time searching for him, there was no chance I was going to walk away.

My pulse pounding in my head, I started slowly down the alley. I went about halfway and stopped. I stood shivering, my breath frosting in front of me as it hit the cold air.

"Hello, Charlie," Waterman said. He had a soft southern twang to his voice.

I had to swallow again before I could answer him. "You're Mr. Waterman."

"That's right."

"And you know me. You know who I am."

He gave a brief, tight smile. "I know you, Charlie. I know who you are. And I know what's happened to you. I can explain everything."

It would be impossible to describe what I felt then. A soaring sense of relief and hope. It was like a gigantic bird of some kind taking flight inside me. Was there really a chance I might be able to stop running, to stop being alone, to stop being afraid? Was there really a chance I could find my life again?

"Tell me," I said. My voice was hoarse. I could barely get the words out. "Tell me everything."

With another slight smile, Waterman shook his head. "I'm sorry," he said. "It's not that easy." He shifted his gaze, looking past me, looking behind me.

I glanced over my shoulder to see what he was looking at. Another man had entered the alley. He was a heavyset man with broad shoulders and a belly that pressed against the front of his gray overcoat. He had an LA Dodgers baseball cap pulled down low over slickly handsome features: thick lips, a Roman nose, sunken eyes.

Confused, I looked back at Waterman, but Waterman went on looking at the man in the Dodgers cap.

Then Waterman said: "Shoot him."

I spun around in time to see the man in the Dodgers cap lift a gun and point it at my chest. In the narrow alley there was nowhere to run, nowhere to hide.

The man pulled the trigger. I heard the gun whisper, saw the smoke, felt the impact in the center of my chest.

And then I was falling and falling into utter blackness.

CHAPTER TWO

Dreams and Whispers

I was home again, a soft pillow under my head, warm and secure with the covers pulled up around my ears. I could hear my mother calling me from the foot of the stairs, telling me it was time for school . . .

But I didn't go to school. I was suddenly walking along Spring River in my hometown of Spring Hill. I was holding Beth's hand. The leaves on the birch trees around us were orange and yellow against the white bark and the wind was stirring in them. Beth's blue eyes were turned up to me. Her curling honey-brown hair moved at the edges of her smooth features as the wind blew. I looked at her and hurt with yearning. We had fallen in love during my trial for Alex's murder. We had fallen in love . . . but I couldn't remember it. I wanted desperately to remember. But it was part of that missing year.

I felt a jolt and suddenly Beth was gone. The river was gone and so were the birch trees. Suddenly I was moving quickly and another guy's face was moving quickly in front of me. Mike—Sensei Mike—my karate teacher. He was throwing blows at me, quick chops and punches, too fast to block. They hit me in the chest and the shoulder, jolting me again and again. Mike's face was as it always was, long and lean with chiseled features under that neatly combed black hair he was so proud of and the big black mustache. But then he opened his mouth to speak—and the voice that came out wasn't his. It was deep and rumbling with a British accent. Somehow I knew it was Winston Churchill's voice, the voice of the man who was British prime minister during World War II. He spoke the words that Mike had taught me, the philosophy he'd taught me: "Never give in; never give in—never, never, never, never, in nothing great or small, large or petty, never give in except to convictions of honor and good sense. Never yield to force: never yield to the apparently overwhelming might of the enemy."

I didn't want to give in, but they were after me. I was in the woods. It was dark. It was pitch-black night. All around me, dogs were howling, sirens were sounding, footsteps were drawing near. It was the Homelanders. The Homelanders were coming for me. The Homelanders was a group run by Islamo-fascist terrorists from the Middle East. They hated . . . Well, they hated a lot of things. They hated our country. They hated the idea that people should be free to choose how they live, to choose what they believe. There were Americans among them too, homegrown traitors they'd recruited because it was easier for them to move around the country, to get at their targets. The Homelanders thought I was one of them, one of their American traitors. Only they thought I had betrayed *them* as well. So they were chasing me, closing in on me, and then . . .

Then suddenly, bright lights blinded me. The night whirled red and blue. I wasn't in the woods anymore. I was on a city street. The police were coming for me. Their cars were racing at me from every street, from every side. They thought I'd killed my best friend, Alex Hauser. I'd been put on trial for it, convicted of it. I'd been put in prison. I'd escaped.

But I couldn't remember any of that. It was like falling in love with Beth. Like falling into league with the Homelanders. It was all part of that missing year, that chunk of memory that had somehow disappeared.

I felt another jolt—and now suddenly they had me. The police. I was captured. Under arrest. In handcuffs. Detective Rose—the man who'd arrested me for Alex's murder, the man who was relentlessly hunting me still— was leading me to a patrol car that would take me back to prison. I was surrounded by state troopers. They were crowded around me, pressing in on every side. The open door of the patrol car was getting closer and closer. They were going to put me in the car and take me back to prison. But now a voice was whispering in my ear:

You're a better man than you know. Find Waterman.

Find Waterman . . .

Suddenly, with another jolt, my eyes came open. I was awake. My heart was pounding—and it pounded faster as I realized I was still in utter blackness.

Am I dead?

That was the first thought that went through my mind. But then there was another jolt. I bounced heavily

14

and felt a throbbing ache in my head. Oh man, it hurt—it hurt like crazy. Well, at least I wasn't dead anyway. Not with a headache like that!

But then, where was I?

I reached out and felt the space around me. Metal. Plastic. Some kind of padding material. Some kind of heavy insulated wires.

I listened. An engine. Rushing wind. Highway noises . . .

With a spurt of claustrophobic panic, it came to me: I was locked in the trunk of a moving car.

My first instinct was to start pounding on the trunk lid, to start shouting, "Help! Let me out! Let me out!" Which would've been pretty dumb, I know. I mean, whoever put me in the trunk of a car probably hadn't done it by accident. They probably weren't walking around, thinking, *Hey, what happened to Charlie? Gee, I hope we didn't leave him in the trunk of the car!* Obviously, they'd dumped me in here on purpose, and so if I started shouting, "Help! Help! Let me out!" they probably wouldn't say, *Oh, okay, sorry, we thought you liked it in there.* All it would do was alert them that I was awake. So, like I say, screaming for help: dumb idea. And I *knew* it was a dumb idea. But still, let me tell you, in my fear and claustrophobia, the urge to start screaming anyway was almost overwhelming. I had to work hard to fight it down. I had to force myself to breathe slowly, deeply. I had to force myself to think. I thought: *Okay, what's my situation? How did I get here? What happened to me?*

Then I remembered: Waterman.

I felt another jolt as the car went over a bump. I flinched as the pain lanced through my head like a jagged bolt of lightning. I winced. I thought: *Ow!* Then I thought: *Waterman*. Right. Waterman in the alley. And the man in the Dodgers cap. And the gun . . .

The gun. The man in the Dodgers cap had shot me. Quickly, my hand went to my chest. I felt the bruise, the stinging pain under my fleece where the gunshot had hit me.

But that's all I felt. No dampness. No blood. Plus I was alive. Which meant I hadn't been shot with a bullet. A bullet to that spot would've almost surely hit my heart, almost surely killed me, with plenty of blood to go around. Flinching at the pain in my head again, I realized: it wasn't a bullet. It was a dart, a drug of some kind. The man in the Dodgers cap had fired a tranquilizer weapon at me. I'd been knocked out, but I was unhurt. I was alive.

Okay. So that was my situation. On the plus side, I was alive. That definitely had to be counted as a positive. In terms of negatives: well, the whole locked-in-the-trunk-of-the-car thing. It was hard to find anything good to say about that.

In fact, as I thought about it, I felt the panic and claustrophobia start to rise up in me again.

Again, I forced myself to breathe deeply. *Never give in*, I told myself. *Never, never, never, never.*

Feeling stiff and uncomfortable, I shifted in the small space. I discovered I had a little room to move. My eyes were adjusting to the darkness now too. I could see that I was facing the rear of the car. I struggled to turn around, to face the front, to see what else I could see. Moving like that redoubled my sense of claustrophobia. Made me feel like I was in a coffin, buried underground, left for dead. Not a pleasant feeling.

All the same, I did manage to make the turn onto my back then onto my other side. When I finished, I could see the barrier between the trunk and the backseat. That gave me an idea. I struggled to get closer to the barrier. I managed to press my ear against it. I listened.

Sure enough, I could hear what was going on inside the car. I could hear voices in there. At first, it was hard to make out the words through the barrier. The rumble of the car's motion kept drowning them out too. But if I lay very still and kept my breathing shallow, I could hear some of what was being said.

"We don't have much choice. One way or another, we've got to act."

That last part came to me clearly. I was pretty sure it was Waterman speaking. I recognized the distinctive southern twang I'd heard in the alley.

Somebody answered him, but the voice was muffled.

Then Waterman said, "No. And it isn't going to be pretty finding out. But I don't see what other options we have. They're close. Very close. We can't just wait and hope for the best."

This time, the answering voice was clearer: "He may still be worth something to us as he is." I guessed it was the guy in the Dodgers cap speaking.

"It's gone too far for that, Jim," said Waterman. "As he is, he can only be a liability."

Again, there was an answer I couldn't hear.

I licked my dry lips, staring into the darkness of the car's trunk. Were they talking about me? Were they deciding what to do with me? I thought they probably were.

Then I heard Waterman say flatly, "Well, then we've got to get rid of him."

There was another jolt, another flash of pain through my skull.

We've got to get rid of him.

That didn't sound good at all.

Now I could feel the car changing direction, slowing. We were getting off the highway. I figured we must be approaching our destination. Was this the place where they were going to get rid of me?

"I don't know," the second speaker—Jim—began. "Either way, I think we have some kind of responsibility—"

"No," said Waterman, cutting him off. "This was part of the deal. We knew it would be like this from the beginning."

After that, the voices stopped for a while. I shifted in the car again. I felt around me, trying to find some way to get the trunk open or maybe some weapon I might be able to use: a tire iron maybe. But there was nothing. The trunk's latch was hidden inside the body of the car. And the only objects around me were those insulated wires, which I now realized were a pair of jumper cables. Not much help.

I'd have to wait and take my chances. They might just open up the trunk and shoot me, but they might take me out first, take me somewhere secluded. Sensei Mike had trained me well in karate. I was a good fighter, a black belt. There might be a chance, a small chance, I could break away from these guys and run for it.

So I said a prayer for calm and for courage and I waited and, while I waited, I tried to think.

Who were they? Who was Waterman? Was he one of the Homelanders? I had no way of knowing. That time I'd been arrested, someone had whispered in my ear that I should "find Waterman," but I didn't know who the whisperer was—a friend or an enemy? If all Waterman wanted was to "get rid" of me, why hadn't he just done it in the alley? Why hadn't he just shot me for real and left me there?

Maybe they need something, I thought. *Maybe they think I have some important piece of information.*

It isn't going to be pretty finding out.

That didn't sound so good either. Were they going to torture me? Did my life depend on the answers I gave them? Didn't they understand? I didn't know what had happened. I didn't remember.

The car went on and on. I felt another turn. The road grew bumpier. I was jostled back and forth roughly in the trunk. It felt like we were on a dirt road. We were heading away from traffic, away from people.

Now I heard the voices in the car start up again. They were easier to hear than before because the car had slowed down to deal with the rough road.

"Where do you want to do this?" said the voice I now knew as Jim.

"Might as well use the Panic Room. That way, we can be sure no one hears the screaming."

Great. Screaming. Screaming was never a positive. And Waterman's tone when he talked about it was chillingly cool and casual. As if torturing me and getting rid of me was just another piece of business that had to be taken care of.

There was a brief silence, then the guy called Jim said, "Poor kid."

"Like I said," Waterman drawled, "this was the deal from the beginning."

"Yeah. Still. Poor kid."

My stomach turned. I was scared, I don't mind saying. I'd escaped from the Homelanders. I'd escaped from the police. But something about these guys was different. They sounded so relaxed, so professional. Their tone sapped my confidence, made me feel there was no chance I could fight my way out of this.

The car slowed. I felt a slight bump as if the car were

lifting over a threshold. The car stopped. The engine died.

I heard the doors opening. I held my breath. I heard footsteps.

Then suddenly, Waterman's voice sounded right nearby, right outside the trunk.

"Let's get this over with," he said.

The trunk came open.

CHAPTER THREE

Milton Two

After such a long time in the darkness, I had to blink and squint in the pale light of evening before I could see anything. Then I saw Waterman, silhouetted by the light, standing above me holding the lid of the car trunk. Jim—the man in the Dodgers cap—was standing just behind him, his hands shoved into his overcoat pockets.

"Come on, Charlie," Waterman said grimly. "Let's go."

He stepped back. I climbed slowly out of the trunk, my limbs stiff and aching after the long confinement.

"Where are we?" I said. "Where are you taking me?"

"Sorry," said Waterman. "You don't get any questions. We ask; you answer. That's how it's going to work."

I stood up, rubbing my legs to bring them back to life. I looked around, blinking, dazed.

We were in an old barn of dried-out brown wood. The fading daylight poured through the open bay doors. Strips of light came in between the cracks in the ancient wallboards. Farm tools hung on nails in the boards: a pitchfork, a shovel, a pair of gardening shears. My eyes went over them as I tried to think of some way to get my hands on something I could use as a weapon.

Waterman seemed to read my mind. "Don't even think about it, son. I know you're a tough guy. But you're not tough enough. This is already going to be unpleasant. Don't make it any harder on yourself than it has to be."

I eyed my two captors. Waterman looked like he was fifty or so. Dodger Jim looked somewhat younger, not much. But both of them looked like they were hard characters, very confident and experienced. It was a pretty good bet that Dodger Jim was holding a gun in his overcoat pocket too, and it might not be a tranquilizer gun this time. If I was going to try to escape, this wasn't the time. I was going to have to take them when they were off guard in order to have even half a chance.

Waterman glanced over his shoulder, as if he was afraid someone might be watching us. Outside the barn door I couldn't see anything but forest.

"All right," he said. He slammed the trunk. "We can't just stand around here. Let's get moving."

Dodger Jim stepped aside and gave an ironic wave of his hand toward the barn door: right this way, sir. I stepped out into a deep forest that was fading into shadow with the coming of night. It was cold here, colder than in the city, colder with every moment the light grew dimmer. My breath frosted in front of me, and I could feel the chill eating at my skin through my fleece.

Waterman closed the barn door and then he and Dodger Jim came up, one on either side of me. There was a trail going off in three directions. We took the path to the right.

Sometimes we walked together. More often, the trail was too narrow and Waterman led the way with me in the middle and Dodger Jim behind me. No chance to make a break.

At first, I kept my mouth shut. I knew Waterman didn't want me asking questions. But then I thought: *What do I care what he wants?* I needed to distract these guys so I could get my chance to strike.

So I asked: "Hey, who are you people anyway?"

Waterman said nothing.

I tried again. "I mean, are you the good guys or the bad guys?"

Waterman snorted. "Doesn't that depend whose side you're on?"

The answer chilled me. I'd heard too much of that kind of talk lately. Nothing is really good or bad, it's all a matter of perspective, it's all a matter of which culture you come from, a matter of what you've been taught and what you happen to believe. It sounded like Mr. Sherman, a history teacher of mine who'd turned out to be one of the Homelanders. It was just the sort of thing he used to say.

I'd had a chance to think about it a lot over the last week or so as I was making my way to New York to find Waterman. I'd had to think about it. When everyone is against you—not just the terrorists but the police too— you have to wonder: Did I do something wrong? Am I the bad guy? Should I turn myself in and take the pun- ishment society says I deserve? It's not like a math quiz or a spelling bee. The answers aren't as black-and-white as that. But that doesn't mean there are no answers—and, in my situation, you have to get them right or it could mean disaster. It could mean you die.

"No," I said. "I don't think good and bad does depend on whose side you're on. I don't think anyone really believes that either. I think they just say it because they think it makes them sound open-minded and sophisticated or something."

"Oh yeah?" Waterman glanced back at me with an ironic smile on his face. "You think there's just good and bad and that's it, huh?"

"Pretty much," I said. "I mean, maybe we don't always know what it is. Maybe we goof up as we're trying to find it. But that doesn't mean it's not there. That doesn't mean you can't get closer to it if you keep trying."

Waterman faced forward again, making his way along the narrow dirt path. "Some people would say that's a pretty simplistic idea of the world."

This was good. I had his attention now. If I could keep him talking, I might find the opportunity to make my move.

"A rock is harder than a feather," I said. "You can talk and jabber and make exceptions, but in the end, if you have to choose which one is gonna hit you in the head, you'll choose the feather every single time."

Up ahead of me, Waterman made a dismissive riffling noise. "What are you talking about? So a rock is harder than a feather. So what? What's that supposed to mean?"

"It means that simple and simplistic aren't the same thing. Some things are true whether they're simple or not. Sometimes people just get complicated so they don't have to stand up for what's simple and true. It's easier. It's safer. But that doesn't make it right."

I glanced behind me. Dodger Jim was there at my back, his hands jammed into his overcoat pockets. His eyes were turning this way and that, scanning the woods, as if he expected someone to leap out at us at any moment. He wasn't listening to our conversation. That was good too. He had the gun. He was the first one I was going to take down.

Waterman didn't look back as he spoke now. "Well, congratulations, Charlie. You know a rock is harder than a feather. I'm happy for you. What else do you know?"

"I know freedom is better than slavery," I said.

"Oh yeah?"

"Yeah."

"How do you know that?"

"Because I know love is better than hate—and you can't love something by force. You can't be forced to love your neighbor or your country or God or anything. No one has the right to force you and they couldn't if they wanted to. You have to be free, so you can choose, even if that means some people choose wrong."

"Wow. You sure know a lot."

"I know a rock is harder than a feather and I know freedom is better than slavery. That's what I know. And that means the people working for freedom are the good guys. So which are you, Mr. Waterman? The good guys or the bad guys?"

Once again, Waterman didn't even bother to turn around. "Well, I still say things are a lot more complicated than—"

That's what he was starting to say when I struck.

I turned fast, snapping the back of my fist at Dodger Jim's head. I gauged the blow perfectly. My knuckles smashed into his temple. His Dodgers cap flew off. His mouth fell open. His eyes seemed to roll in his head. For an instant, he was stunned.

I used that instant. I seized his right arm and yanked it out of his pocket. Sure enough, he had the gun clutched in his hand even now. I twisted his wrist with one hand and yanked the weapon from his loose fingers with the other.

It all took no more than a second or two, but by then,

Waterman was on the move. He'd sensed the action behind him, heard the blow, and turned to come after me. He only got a single step. Then I leveled the gun at his chest.

"Hold it right—!" I started to say.

There was a sizzling white flash. A searing pain shot from my wrist up through my arm. I cried out. My arm spasmed, out of my control. The muscles went dead and the gun flew from my limp fingers, twirling blackly through the evening air. The burning blow knocked me off my feet. The next thing I knew I was lying on my back in the dirt, staring upward, dumb and dazed.

Something was hovering over me in the twilight, something just hanging there in midair, staring down at me. At first, in my stupefied state, I thought it must be some kind of magical bird or something. What else could just hover in the air like that? But as my head cleared, I saw it was a machine of some sort. It was about the size and shape of an Xbox controller. It was camouflaged like an army uniform. It had a red light burning on it. There seemed to be a round lens in the center of it: that staring eye.

I started to get up, shifting to the side. As I did, the flying thing also darted to the side, following my movements.

"I wouldn't do anything too sudden if I were you,"

Waterman drawled above me. "That thing can do a lot of damage."

I believed him. I moved more slowly, rubbing the raw, red spot on my wrist where the thing had blasted me. The muscles of my arm were starting to come back to life with a dull throb of pain.

"What is it?" I said thickly, gesturing with my head toward the hovering machine.

"That," Waterman told me, "is Milton Two. He's our security drone. He let you off easy. He can dial that electronic pulse up high enough to knock you straight into eternity. Releases tear gas too when it has a mind. Pretty cool, huh?"

"Yeah," I said sourly. "Great."

The thing buzzed and hovered and shifted, following my every move as I started to climb to my feet. But I didn't get far. Just as I propped my hand against the gritty earth to push myself up, another blow struck me. This one hit me in the side, right near the floating rib. It knocked the wind right out of me. Groaning, I fell, face-first, back to the dirt.

For a moment I thought I'd drawn Milton Two's fire again. But no, it wasn't the drone this time. It was Dodger Jim. He'd kicked me.

"That's for the hit in the head," he said, towering above me where I lay. Then he grabbed me by the collar and hauled me roughly to my feet.

He had his cap back on. He had his gun back too. He jammed it hard against the side of my head. With his free hand, he rubbed the spot on his temple where I'd clocked him.

"Try that again," he said nastily. "See what happens."

"All right, Jim," said Waterman. "That's enough. You can't blame the kid for trying." He was looking around the woods nervously. "Let's get out of the open already."

Dodger Jim gave me an angry shove down the trail. I looked at him. I looked at Milton Two, zipping around me in the twilight. I didn't have much choice. I started walking.

Waterman and Dodger Jim both fell in line behind me. The small drone flew along at my side, watching me the whole time, ready to blast me if I tried another move. None of them was taking any chances now.

Wherever we were going, whatever was going to happen, whatever they were going to do to me, there was no escape.

CHAPTER FOUR

The Bunker

We walked on down the trail. The cold grew sharper as the light continued to bleed out of the gray sky. The branches of the trees became gnarling black shapes around us. The forest began to disappear into the night.

But then, strangely, the twilight seemed to reverse itself. It became easier to see the trail in front of me. I realized the forest around me was growing thinner, the trees sparser. We were entering a clearing—that's why there was more light.

We stepped out of a cluster of tall pines—and I

stopped, staring, my lips parted in surprise. I heard my two captors stop behind me as well. The drone—Milton Two—stopped flying and hovered in midair next to my head.

We were standing at the edge of what had once been—I don't know what—an enormous building maybe—maybe a compound made up of a lot of buildings. Whatever it had been, it was all in ruins now. Long barracks stood dark and empty, their windows shattered, the last glass in their frames jagged, broken. Taller structures rose and then fell away in a shambles. Columns stood free here and there. Rooms stood roofless, the doors torn away to reveal the interior. All around, the forest was moving back in to reclaim the space. Vines twisted down the broken walls. New young trees sprang up, breaking through old tiles and floorboards.

Even as I stood staring at it, the ruins faded into the deepening dusk. The first tendrils of a forest mist curled along the ground, coiled around the structures, giving the place an eerie, ghostly atmosphere.

"Keep moving," said Dodger Jim. He prodded me roughly in the back with his gun. He was still angry about that shot to the head.

I walked forward, the mist parting before my feet.

"What is this place?" I said.

"It used to be a psychiatric facility," Waterman answered. "They built it out here to keep the inmates away from the locals. Now it's empty—except for us."

The ruined, misty buildings surrounded me as I went on. I looked around, half expecting to see people—or other creatures—darting here and there between the structures. Sometimes I thought I caught a movement at the corner of my eye, but when I turned, there was nothing. It was—or at least I thought it was—only my imagination.

"Over here," said Waterman.

Now he came around in front of me again. He knew I was no danger to him anymore. With that drone following my every move, ready to blast me if I tried anything—and with Dodger Jim eager for the chance to get some payback for that strike to the head—I didn't stand a chance.

Waterman led the way confidently through the maze of broken, vine-covered walls. We moved toward the center of the compound. Up ahead, I made out what looked like the remains of a tower, a cylinder rising black against the surrounding darkness. As we got closer, I saw that its brick walls were crawling with ivy. It had no roof.

The cylinder just ended in broken jags about ten feet above my head. Down below, where the door had been, there was now just an uneven opening.

Waterman stepped through that opening, disappearing inside.

I hesitated. I had the feeling that once I went into this place, I would never come out again.

Once more, Dodger Jim prodded me with the barrel of his gun.

"Move it," he said.

I glanced back at him. He grinned at me, his eyes shining in the dark. He was waiting for me to strike at him. Ready this time. Milton Two hovered in the air just above me like a deadly hummingbird, its single eye trained on me.

"Yeah," said Dodger Jim. "You have something to say?"

What could I do? I shook my head. I turned and stepped through the door into the tower.

There was nothing inside. Just an empty circular room with brick walls and a concrete floor. There was a winding stair leading upward, but it ended abruptly on a broken step, going nowhere.

Waterman waited for me to enter—then we both waited for Dodger Jim. When we were all inside, Waterman approached the wall. He began to move his hand over the bricks. He kept his fingers spread, the palm held out as he traced a complex pattern in the air, difficult to follow. It reminded me of a party magician making hocus-pocus passes over a handkerchief before making a rabbit appear.

But there was no rabbit. Instead, I heard a low buzzing noise. The wall began to open under Waterman's hand.

There was a door hidden in the wall. A rectangle of bricks was sliding aside in a controlled electronic motion. Then, with a metallic *thunk*, it stopped. The door stood opened into blackness.

Waterman gestured to the opening.

"Go on."

I moved to the black rectangle and peered in. From here, I could make out a narrow platform in front of a shadowy flight of metal stairs.

One more time, I looked up at Waterman. I searched his eyes, trying to guess who he was, what he wanted, whose side he was on. There was nothing there. His expression was sardonic and distant and impossible to read. He held his hand out and waited.

I stepped into the opening, onto the platform, then onto the stairs. I started down.

It was not a long descent, just an ordinary single flight into a deep cellar. A very dim security lamp was burning yellow at the bottom, giving just enough light for me to make my way.

I reached the bottom. The narrow flight opened out here into a small semicircular anteroom. There was no other entry or exit besides the stairs. Nothing but a blank metal wall.

The next moment, Waterman was down the stairs as well, standing next to me. Once again, he reached out and moved his palm over the face of the wall. He made the same pattern. I tried to follow it. I thought it might come in handy later if I ever got a chance to escape. I watched his hand make out a series of diagonals, then a series of straight lines—a square maybe?—then another diagonal. It was too complicated to remember. Again, when he was finished, there was a buzzing, grinding noise.

A door swung open and bright light flooded out.

After the forest twilight and the descent, the light hurt my eyes. I squinted against it, holding up my hand for protection. Meanwhile, a voice reached me from inside the brightness. It was a voice I recognized.

It said, "Charlie West is an extremely dangerous young man."

Startled, I glanced at Waterman. "Rose!"

It was Detective Rose, the policeman who had arrested me for the murder of Alex Hauser.

When Waterman didn't answer, I stepped quickly through the doorway into the light. There he was: Rose. His face was on a monitor on the wall in front of me, hanging above my head.

I remembered the guy only too well. He was a short, trim, round-faced black man with flat features and a thin mustache. It was his eyes you remembered mostly. Smart, cold eyes that always seemed to be calculating, thinking, considering. You looked in those eyes and you knew: he was a man with a purpose. Unfortunately, that purpose was to hunt me down, to bring me to what he thought was justice. He had believed I was innocent at first, and when he'd decided I was guilty, he'd never forgiven me for fooling him. He was embarrassed by the fact that I had escaped from prison too, escaped from him. He would never give up hunting me. He would never rest until he caught me.

"He's trained in karate." Rose went on speaking on the monitor. "And by all accounts, he's extremely skilled. Civilians should not approach him, even if they're armed. I can't emphasize this enough. This man is vicious. He's already been convicted of one murder, and now we have every reason to believe he's committed a second."

"What?" I said.

I was so taken aback that I didn't even notice my new surroundings. I just went on staring at the television monitor as Detective Rose's face was replaced by a snapshot of Mr. Sherman, my old history teacher. Recently, I had discovered that it was Sherman who had recruited me to join the Homelanders. He was the one who had killed Alex Hauser when Alex tried to leave the organization. Then he had framed me for the murder in order to make me angry at American injustice so I would sign on with him and his Islamo-fascist allies to attack the country.

I knew that Sherman was in trouble with the Homelanders. Their leader, a man who called himself Prince, felt that when Sherman had recruited me, he had brought a traitor into the ranks. Sherman had tried to capture me at gunpoint in order to prove himself to Prince. I had knocked him out—knocked him out, yes, but I hadn't killed him. He was alive the last time I saw him.

Apparently, he was not alive anymore.

"The gruesome remains of the history teacher were found in an abandoned house at the outskirts of the little city," a newswoman's voice was saying. Sherman's face faded out and was replaced by a picture of the old haunted McKenzie mansion where I had hidden out the last time I was home. Was it only a couple of weeks ago? The newswoman went on, "Police say Sherman was tortured before he was killed."

The images disappeared as the monitor went blank.

"That was on the news about forty-five minutes ago."

I looked down at the voice. I saw I was in a long, low-ceilinged cellar of a room with white plaster walls and a couple of doors leading off into other rooms. The fluorescent lighting gave the room a bright, cold, sterile feeling. The place was packed with equipment. There were workstations along the walls with laptops set up on them. There were several monitors hanging up high on the walls. Each monitor had pictures broken up into several little squares, as if it was bringing in several video feeds at once. Each laptop had readouts working on the screen. I was too dazed and confused to take it all in.

"They're warning people that he could be heading for Manhattan. They seem to be hot on his trail."

The guy who was speaking was a young man, American of Asian descent. He was trim with a squarish head, a strangely cheerful face—it seemed strange under the

41

circumstances anyway. He was dressed in a shirt and tie, but no jacket. He was sitting at one of the workstations, one of the laptops. He was holding a small rectangular object in one hand. At first, I thought it was an iPhone.

"This is Milton One," said Waterman with his ironic drawl. "The inventor and operator of Milton Two."

Milton One held up the iPhone-thing and waggled it around. I could see a video readout on it. The little gadget was the control for the security drone upstairs.

"Sorry to blast you, kid," he said merrily. "But it sure was fun. I've been dying to try this thing out under battle conditions."

With that reminder, the pain of the burn on my wrist came back to me. I rubbed the spot.

"Glad to be of service," I muttered.

Now, hearing the conversation, a woman came into the room, entering a step through the doorway to my right. She was spindly and crow-faced with black hair streaked with gray, pulled back tight. She had hard brown eyes empty of emotion. She had a nasty scowl plastered on her face.

"Get ready," Waterman told her.

She nodded once and disappeared through the doorway again without a word.

Now Waterman turned his attention back to me. "You heard Rose, Charlie. The police are saying you killed Sherman now."

"I didn't kill him," I said angrily. I was frustrated by the injustice of it. I couldn't remember Alex dying. Until I got the truth out of Sherman, I sometimes worried I might really have killed him. But I *did* remember what happened with Sherman. "He was alive when I left him, I swear it. The Homelanders must have found him. They must've punished him for letting me get away. I can't believe Detective Rose is blaming that on me too."

Waterman answered with a slight sniff. I couldn't tell what he was thinking. "We're going to find out all about that," he said. "We're both going to find out all about everything."

That didn't sound good. I felt a nauseating gout of fear as I wondered what was coming next.

"What's that supposed to mean?" I said.

Without answering, Waterman walked across the room to an empty spot on the wall underneath one of the monitors and in between two of the workstations. Once more, he moved his palm over the space. Once more, I tried to follow the movement, the pattern of diagonals and straight lines. It reminded me of something, but I couldn't place it.

Once more, as he finished, there was the hum of a motor. A door that had been invisible swung open. A light came on automatically within the next room.

Waterman gestured to the opening.

"Welcome to the Panic Room," he said.

CHAPTER FIVE

The Panic Room

I took a deep breath, trying to stay calm. No way I wanted to go through that door, to go into that place. But I was surrounded. There was no getting out of it.

I walked into the Panic Room.

It was a small, square, stark space. Looked like a prison cell. Four white walls, a metal chest against one wall, a cot against another, a metal toilet, a metal sink, a metal chair in the center of the floor.

I didn't like the metal chair especially. Just the sight of it sent a new pulse of fear through me. It reminded me of how all this had started. I'd gone to bed one night and awakened strapped to a metal chair just like that one. Two Homelander goons had been torturing me. There were so many memories I wished I could get back, but that was one memory I wished I could get rid of forever.

Waterman and Dodger Jim came into the room behind me. Dodger Jim made a motion with his hand, and the electric door swung shut, becoming an invisible part of the wall again. I felt light-headed in the small space, helpless to stop what was happening.

Waterman stood to my right. Dodger Jim was to my left, holding the gun on me.

"This is the way it is, Charlie," Waterman said. There was no tone, no emotion to his voice at all now. "We're going to handcuff you to that chair . . ."

The fear flared higher. "Why? What for? Who are you people?" I said.

"Shut up," said Dodger Jim.

"Either you can just sit down and let us do it, or we can do it by force," said Waterman. "Whichever you choose, the result is going to be the same."

I took a deep breath. I nodded, as if I agreed with him. And the fact was: I knew he was probably right. But I didn't care whether he was right or not. There was just no way on this planet I was going to let them hand-cuff me to that chair without a fight. Once I was there, it was over. Once they had me cuffed, I had no chance at all.

"Look," I said, "if you have something to ask me, why don't you just ask? I have nothing to hide."

"We have to be sure," said Waterman. "Get in the chair, Charlie."

I put my hands up as if to surrender. "Okay," I said.

Then I pivoted, fast, and sent a snapping roundhouse kick at Dodger Jim's gun hand.

The gun went flying—and then Waterman was on me. He was big, fast, tough—and a real fighter. I tried to chop at his throat, but he blocked it hard and got my arm in a lock. He got his foot behind me and, as he hit me in the chest with his hand, his foot came swinging back and swept my feet out from under me.

I flew backward, landing hard on the floor. I gave a loud "Oof!" as the wind rushed out of me. In the next instant, Waterman was on top of me, his hand clutching my throat, squeezing off the airway. I couldn't breathe. The world went watery in front of my eyes.

The next thing I knew, Waterman and Dodger Jim were dragging me to my feet. They hurled me into the chair, hard. Dodger Jim punched me in the jaw. It felt like getting hit by a brick.

My head flew back, and my mind seemed to fall away from the world like falling down a well.

"Knock it off," I heard Waterman say from a distance.

"I told him what would happen if he tried me again," said Dodger Jim.

My head slumped forward. I was only half-conscious as they held my arms against the arms of the metal chair and snapped the handcuffs around my wrists.

The two men stood back, breathing hard. I looked up at them from the chair, helpless.

Dodger Jim shook his head angrily, rubbing the spot on his wrist where I'd kicked him. "You're a tough little monkey, kid," he said. "I'll give you that."

The door in the wall buzzed and opened. The crow-faced woman came in. My eyes went wide in terror as I saw she was carrying a syringe.

That woke me up. I jolted back in the chair as if there was some chance of getting away from her. I struggled against the handcuffs, trying uselessly to get free.

Waterman stood in front of me. "Listen to me, Charlie," he said. "Listen. You have to listen. We're not your enemies, so help me."

It was a long moment before I could still my panic and stop trying to break through the handcuffs.

"We have to do this," Waterman said. "We have no choice. The Homelanders are close. Very close. They've hacked some of our files. We don't know how many. We don't know how much they know. But they know about me. They've been watching me for weeks. It's only a matter of time before they find this place and strike and try to kill us all. We want to help you, but we have to be sure you're still on our side and there's only one way to do that. You've been out of touch for too long. You might have gone over. The loss of memory . . . everything . . . it might all be a fake, or there might be permanent damage that makes you a liability. We just can't trust you until we know for sure."

"Who are you?" I said hoarsely. "What are you talking about? Who are you?"

"We're the good guys, Charlie. If liberty is better than slavery, like you said—if the people who work for liberty are the good guys—then we're the good guys, though we can't always be as good as we might like. The Islamo-fascists don't believe in freedom at all, Charlie, believe me. They want everyone to think the same thing, to do what they're told. They hate our country, our liberty, our Constitution. Our whole way of life. And the Americans who've joined them, who've kidded themselves into thinking they're no worse than us, that one philosophy is no better than another, are self-hating fools. They're your enemies, Charlie."

"If you're on my side, why are you doing this to me?" I shouted at him, struggling against the handcuffs again.

"I'm sorry, but we have to be sure where you stand," Waterman said. He nodded at the crow-faced woman with the syringe. She stepped toward the chair as I struggled to get away from her.

"The Homelanders are going to attack this country, Charlie," Waterman said. "They're going to hit us soon, hard, and from the inside. The people in this bunker are some of the only people left who can stop them. If they get to us, then we've got no chance. We can't risk the possibility that you're their agent."

The crow-faced woman nodded at Dodger Jim. He came forward and grabbed my left arm, rolling up my sleeve to bare the vein for the needle. He was grinning.

"You're not gonna like this, kid," he said with vengeance gleaming in his eyes. "It hurts like crazy."

"Listen to me, Charlie," said Waterman. "If we haven't lost you, you're our best hope. If we have, you're our worst enemy. We have to know which it is."

Dodger Jim held my arm. The crow-faced woman lifted the syringe and squirted a drop or two of clear fluid from the needle.

"We're going to give you something that will make you remember," said Waterman. "I wish I could say it was going to be painless, but it's not. I wish I could say it was going to be instantaneous, but it's going to take time. Still, in the end, everything that has happened will come back to you. And then you'll know who you are. And then we'll be able to know too."

Now the crow-faced woman lowered the needle to my arm.

I felt as if I had come full circle. Months ago, I had woken up strapped to a chair with a Homelander thug about to inject me with a fluid that they threatened would drive me into agonies and finally kill me. Now, after running and fighting and trying everything I knew to escape, I was back again in the same place, in the same predicament. Only this time, the injection was coming from the good guys—or so they said, at least. This time, the people doing it wanted to save this country instead of destroy it, wanted to defend liberty instead of exterminating it. This time, the torture wasn't a threat, it was a promise: there would be agony, yes, but instead of killing me, it would give me my memory back, give me my life back. I would remember at last how I had gotten here, what I was doing, who I was.

The crow-faced woman pressed the point of the needle against my arm.

"Wait!" I shouted. "Wait!"

She hesitated.

I looked up at Waterman. "This is going to give me my memory back?" I asked him.

He nodded. "It will."

"I'll remember everything? Everything that's happened?"

"It'll take time, but eventually yes, you will."

I took a deep breath, trying to steady myself. This was what I wanted, after all. This was why I had come all this way, searching for Waterman in the first place. If it was going to be painful, well, then, it was going to be painful. That was just the way it was. I was going to have to live with it.

"Give me a second," I said.

Waterman thought about it. Then he nodded at the crow-faced woman. She straightened, taking the syringe away from my arm.

I closed my eyes. *Help me*, I prayed. *Help me to be strong. Help me not to be afraid. Help me to do what you want me to do. And whatever happens, stay with me.*

I opened my eyes. I looked at Waterman. He looked down at me grimly.

"Do it," I said.

The woman drove the needle into my arm.

PART II

CHAPTER SIX

Agony and Remembrance

The pain hit me instantly. It spread through my veins like acid and then filled my body like a raging flame. I tried to hold back my screams, but it was impossible. There was nothing left of me but the fire of pain and my body was pulled tight against the handcuffs and the screams came out of me against my will, wrenched from my chest by the agony.

And then . . . then . . . Well, what happened then was about as weird an experience as I'd ever had—and I have had some weird ones for certain.

Just as I thought I couldn't take it anymore, just as it seemed I was going to die from the pain alone . . . just then . . . it seemed I sort of separated myself from my body. I don't know how else to describe it. My body was there—hurled backward in the chair, all my muscles straining, my mouth open, the screams pouring out of me—but I couldn't feel it anymore. I—the mind I, the soul I—was drifting away from that tormented figure. What was happening to it there in the chair began to seem distant, meaningless. The real me was slipping off into darkness . . . then deeper into darkness . . . leaving behind the pain-racked Charlie in the chair . . . leaving him further and further behind while the blackness engulfed me . . . Finally, the body-Charlie was gone . . . there was only me, this other me, in the darkness and then, up ahead of me in the distance . . . a circle of light . . .

The circle grew bigger . . . bigger . . . It was coming toward me . . . and now . . .

I stepped through it . . .

At first, I only heard voices:

"So you did see Alex last night?"

"Yes. Like I said."

"And you argued with him?"

"Yeah. I guess you could call it that. He argued with me anyway."

Then I saw. I was standing at the edge of a small room with dingy white soundproofing on the walls. There was a video camera hanging in one corner. It stared down at three people sitting at a small table and . . .

Weirder and weirder and weirder. Weird to the point of super-weirdness. Because now, to my amazement, I saw that one of those people sitting at the table was me. Right: I was standing at the edge of the room watching— and what I was watching was myself sitting at the small table. And if that sounds bizarre, believe me, it was.

The person sitting next to me at the table was my dad. Sitting across from us was none other than Detective Rose.

So now I knew where I was—where and when. This was the interrogation room of the police station in my hometown of Spring Hill. It was the day after Alex's murder, the first day I couldn't remember. Only I *was* remembering it. Or at least I was seeing it—seeing it happen right there in front of me.

As soon as I'd heard about Alex's murder, I had told my dad about how I'd seen him the night before and how we'd gone for a drive together. Alex had been angry because he'd heard I was getting friendly with Beth and he and Beth had had sort of a thing for a while. He was angry about that and about a lot of other things too.

Anyway, my dad had taken me to the police station to see Detective Rose, who was investigating the murder.

All this was stuff Beth had told me. But now I was remembering for myself. Not just remembering, but actually seeing what happened right in front of my eyes.

"What did you argue about?" Rose said, talking to the me who was at the table. His voice wasn't friendly or unfriendly. The flat features of his face weren't mean or nice. His eyes were watchful, that's all. He seemed to be studying my face as I answered him, searching it for any signs that would reveal whether I was lying or telling the truth.

I watched me too. It was strange to see myself from a distance like that—to see myself as I was a year ago. I was about six feet tall, thin but with broad shoulders and a lot of muscle def from all the karate and workouts I did. My face was lean and serious with moppy brown hair falling over the forehead. My eyes looked innocent, open, honest, direct, and unafraid. I wondered if they looked the same today.

I—the me in the past—shrugged at Rose's question.

"We argued about . . . stuff, you know. Alex was feeling bad about his folks getting divorced. He and his mom were having money problems and things. He was having all kinds of doubts about . . . you know, life, his faith, the things he believed in. He said he had some new friends who were telling him that everything he'd learned in the past was all untrue. I guess we argued about that too."

"He said he had new friends?" said Rose. "Did he tell you who these new friends were?"

I shook my head. Back then, I had no idea what Alex was talking about. Now I knew that one of his "friends" was Mr. Sherman, the history teacher. I knew that Sherman had taken advantage of Alex's unhappiness and un-certainty and used them to recruit him into the Home-landers. But our conversation that night had convinced Alex that he'd been making a mistake. He tried to pull out of the Homelanders—and Sherman stabbed him to death so he couldn't reveal the organization's existence.

As I say, I knew all that now, but the scene I was watching took place a year ago, and the Charlie I was watching had no clue what was going on.

"All right, so you argued," Rose said to him—said to me, I mean, "and then Alex ran into the park."

"Yeah," I told him. "I tried to stop him . . ."

"But you didn't follow him?"

"No. I knew he didn't want to talk to me anymore. I just went home."

"So you're telling me you weren't even aware he was murdered in the park just a few minutes after he walked away from you?"

"Of course I wasn't aware of it. I didn't hear about it until this morning. Believe me, if I was aware of it, I wouldn't have kept it secret."

"And you don't know why he was whispering your name when he died?"

"No. No. I wish I did."

Well, just in case things weren't weird enough—what with me watching from the sidelines and the younger me sitting at the table—things now got even weirder. Because now, while I was still in two places at once, suddenly, I could actually *feel* what the younger me was feeling, experience what he was experiencing. I felt his sorrow—my sorrow—at Alex's death. I felt his guilt—my guilt—about fighting with Alex the last time we'd been together. I felt confusion about what had happened afterward. Now it was as if I was watching the scene and living it at the same time.

I saw my younger self turn to my father. I saw my

father give me a small smile, a small wink. "It's all right," he said quietly. "Don't worry about anything. Just tell the truth and you'll be fine."

Again, it was as if I was living through two experiences at once. I felt my younger self reassured by my dad's presence. I knew my dad would protect me, that he'd make sure the police didn't make any mistakes. And at the same time, I wished I could reach out from where I was and touch his shoulder, get him to turn to me, get him to see that I was still there, still alive. I missed him. I missed my mom too. I wanted to tell them that, tell them that I missed my life so much and was trying so hard to find my way back to them.

"Would you be willing to give us a DNA sample . . . ?" Detective Rose was saying at the table.

But as he spoke, I felt myself being pulled away from him, pulled back into the darkness beyond the edge of the scene, back and back . . .

Then, suddenly, horribly, there was nothing but pain again, nothing but the coiling, fiery snake of pain lashing and thrashing and biting inside me. For a single, agonized instant, I was in the chair again in the Panic Room . . .

And then, again, I—the soul I—was drifting free . . .

I was standing on a sidewalk, outside a movie theater. It was nighttime. The show must've just been over. People were coming out the doors, back into the street. I could hear the murmur of their voices as they talked about the show.

I looked around me. I knew this place. It was a dingy old theater out near the airport. They played older films here, films that had left the first-run theaters closer to the center of town. Kids only came to this theater when they wanted to get away from the usual crowd, like when they wanted to go on a date and not run into any of their friends.

I watched the people coming out of the movie. I knew what I was going to see a second before I saw it—I knew who I was going to see too: me. Me and Beth—we were about to come out onto the sidewalk together.

We had been seeing each other for a while now, meeting out by the river to walk together and talk. Because of Alex's murder, it somehow didn't feel right for us to go out on an ordinary date. But finally we had. We had come here. We had come to see the movie—or at least to be alone together in the dark theater.

And now I saw us, trailing out behind the rest of the people.

Beth had told me about this too. But she hadn't told me about how nervous I was. She couldn't have because she hadn't known. But just like in the interrogation room, I could feel the scene inside me even as I witnessed it outside me. And the nervousness was huge. Unbelievable. I was practically terrified about what I was going to say.

As I stood there watching, the younger me slipped his hand into Beth's hand. Amazingly, even as I watched from the edge of the scene, I felt the warmth of her palm against mine, the grip of her fingers. And suddenly . . . suddenly, I felt more than that. Suddenly, I felt the love for her flooding into my heart. I was remembering. Finally, finally. I was remembering how much I loved her. It overrode the nervousness I felt. It overrode everything. It welled up in me like a rising tide and all I wanted to do was tell her about it.

Beth and I walked together along the sidewalk, through shadows and pools of light thrown down by the street-lamps. I stood and watched from the sidelines, feeling her hand in mine, feeling the incredible nervousness and fear of telling her what I was about to tell her. Would I be able to find the right words? How would she respond? I knew she was too kind to laugh at me or say anything cruel. But would she shake her head? Would she turn away?

We reached her car. She stood with her back to it, facing me. I looked down at her. We were in deep shadow, but I was close enough to see her eyes. Her blue eyes. Her gentle eyes.

"What were you going to say?" I heard her ask me—and as I stood on the edge of the scene watching, I felt the warmth and sweetness of her breath as she spoke—it was like I was in two places at the same time, inside the scene and observing it from the outside. "Before the movie started," Beth went on, "I said it felt a little wrong for us to be there and you said, 'I feel . . .,' and then you didn't finish. What were you going to say? Do you remember?"

I could feel my past self working up his courage, trying to keep his voice steady so he didn't sound squeaky like some dumb little kid. It felt like the scariest moment of my life up to that time.

"Yeah, I remember," I told Beth. "I was going to say: I feel like nothing about you and me being together is wrong. I feel like when we're together, it's just right, like it's supposed to happen. It's weird too because it's not like in the movies with music playing or fireworks or—or anything that I expected. It's just like . . . I don't know, like a little click, like—You ever do jigsaw puzzles? And you find the right piece and it clicks in? It feels like that."

Beth said, "It feels like that to me too."

Then I kissed her. I felt her lips against my lips, the softness of her as I put my arms around her and pulled her to me.

Standing on the edge of the scene, I closed my eyes and it felt as if I and my past self were melding into one, that I was there again, with Beth in my arms again. It felt so good to remember, finally to remember the sweet ache of loving her . . .

Then I opened my eyes and . . .

Beth was gone. The street was gone. For a moment, I felt heartbroken, missing the touch of her lips on mine. But then I saw . . .

I was at home. In my room. My old room! I couldn't believe it. I was so glad to see it, so glad to be back. There were my karate trophies on the shelf! My *Lord of the Rings* poster on the wall! My bed, my desk . . .

And me! Sitting there, at my desk. Doing my calculus homework, poking numbers into the calculator set beside the computer keyboard, working out a differential equation. Or trying to. Because I couldn't. I couldn't concentrate on the equation at all. All I could think about was Beth.

I had Schoolyard up on my computer screen. It was a

program my high school had that let students IM and e-mail and update one another and hand in homework and get teachers' comments and stuff like that. Normally I didn't go on it much. Everyone could see you were there and IM you and it was pretty distracting, so I stayed off so only my close friends could IM me, which was distracting enough. But Beth liked to go on and talk to her friends, so I went on to talk to her.

That was pretty much all I wanted to do now. Talk to her. I mean, I knew I needed to get that calc homework in by tomorrow, but . . . it was such a good, giddy, happy feeling to be trading messages with her. Even standing there on the outside of the scene, watching the younger me at my desk, I could feel that happiness inside me. I could feel how in love with her I was and how good it felt to know that she was in love with me. And I was so glad that I could finally remember, that it was all coming back, all of it.

I remembered how everything—even Alex's murder—faded into the background of our lives as Beth and I discovered the depths of our feelings for one another. We were together every moment we could find, walking, talking, laughing, feeling like we had stumbled on the whole point of our lives and that that point was for the two of us to be together, to find each other, like two halves of a single person that were created to snap into place.

As I stood there, watching my younger self—wishing I could be back in his body, in his world, in that past, happy life—I looked over his shoulder and saw a new message appear on the monitor.

Beth: *i don't think it's fair, that's all.*

My younger self tapped back at the keyboard: *y not talk to her?*

Beth: *and say what? "Hey, I'm a much better writer than that grade you gave me?"*

I tapped back: *sure, y not? you want me to?*

Beth: *no!!!!!!*

And me: *why so many !!!?*

Beth: *cuz I no what yer like, CW. no karate chopping my eng teacher!*

My younger self and I both laughed.

Then my younger self and I both stopped laughing. Just as we were about to tap an answer to Beth into the keyboard, the monitor went completely black.

My younger self blinked, startled. "Oh, no," he said aloud. He slapped the side of the monitor. "Come on!"

He—I—was beginning to jiggle the On/Off switch at the base of the monitor when the screen crackled in a strange way and a message rolled across the bottom of it. The message was in white letters on the dark background.

It said: *Open your cell phone, Charlie.*

With that, the monitor flashed back on again. There was the Schoolyard home page with the last message from Beth still there, just as before.

Puzzled, I—the younger me—looked around and saw my cell phone lying on the desk, at the opposite end of the keyboard from my calculator. I picked it up. It wasn't ringing or anything. There didn't seem to be anyone there. All the same, I shrugged and opened it as the message directed.

Instantly, a man's voice said: "If you want to know who killed Alex Hauser, come to the Morgan Reservoir in half an hour."

"What?" I said. "Who is this?"

"Come alone. Don't tell anyone."

"How do you know who killed Alex? Who am I talking to?"

"If you tell anyone, I'll know. Do you understand me? I'll know and I won't show up."

"Wait, listen . . . ," I began.

"Do you understand me?"

The younger me looked around the room as if searching for help. Finally, I raised my hand in a gesture of surrender. "Yeah. Yeah, I understand you, sure."

"Do you want to know who killed Alex or not?"

"Yes, of course I do, but . . ."

There was no click, but the silence at the other end of the line became somehow suddenly more complete.

"Hello?" I said. "Hello?"

No answer. The mysterious man was gone.

The present me stood at the edge of the scene, at the edge of my old room at home, watching the past me as he sat there wondering what to do. I didn't know what was going to happen next, but I wanted to call out to myself, to warn myself, to say: *Don't do it. Don't go. Stay where you are. Answer Beth's message, stay with Beth, love Beth, have your life.*

But at the same time, I thought that I could feel what was going through the heart and mind of the past me; I could feel his curiosity, his desire to find Alex's murderer and clear himself of any possible suspicion . . . and I could feel something else too. I could feel his sense of adventure. His need for excitement. His burning ambition to get out of his small-town life and do something important and thrilling and dangerous. I was already planning to try to get into the Air Force Academy. I had even gotten my mom to let me take some flying lessons by way of preparation. But I couldn't apply to the academy until next year. This was now.

I—the present me—wanted to reach out and stop the old me, but I couldn't. All at once, I was fading away from the scene, helplessly drawn back out of my room, back and back into . . .

Nothing. Blackness. Where was I now?

My room was gone. The trophies, the poster on the wall, the computer, my former self. It had all vanished.

And suddenly, I was scared. Very scared. I was alone in the darkness and now there was . . . something . . . a noise . . . an awful noise . . . someone screaming . . . terrible screaming in the distance . . . And I knew: it was me, it was me, in the chair in the Panic Room, screaming in pain . . .

I didn't want to go back there, back to that room, back to that chair, back to that agony.

I turned this way and that, looking for another way out.

There . . . up ahead . . . a dim gray light . . .

I moved toward it.

Now I was on a street. No, a country road. It was

night. Dark. No streetlights, no houses. Somewhere in the distance, a dog was barking.

I looked around, confused. I saw a sparkle, very faint—the stars on water. My eyes began to adjust. I recognized this place. Reservoir Road, up in the wooded hills above my hometown. I could see a hill of dark trees rising up against the night sky to my right, a sandy slope falling away to my left. There was the Morgan Reservoir at the bottom of the slope, the water glinting in the starlight.

I looked around. I half expected to see myself—my younger self—as I had seen him before. But he was nowhere to be found. I was alone. I looked down and . . .

What was this? I wasn't wearing my fleece anymore. I was wearing a windbreaker. I could feel the brisk air of early autumn on me.

Slowly, I lifted my hands, touched my cheeks, felt my hair. I understood.

I didn't see my younger self because I *was* my younger self. I had become my own memory.

The fear, then, was all mine. I knew why I was afraid too. I was here to meet the man behind the mysterious voice on my phone.

If you want to know who killed Alex Hauser . . .

Before, back in the safety of my room, I'd been excited by those words, excited at the prospect of this mysterious meeting, at the idea that I might possibly solve Alex's murder. But now, now that I was actually out here, out here alone in the dark with no one knowing where I was—now suddenly it occurred to me: what a knucklehead I'd been! What an unbelievably stupid idea it was to come out here to meet some voice on the phone without even letting anyone know I was doing it! I mean, didn't I think? Didn't I realize? There was only one person who could possibly know who had killed Alex—and that was the murderer himself! And the only reason the murderer would want me to come out and meet him on an empty road in the middle of the night . . .

Well, let's just say visions of autopsy scenes from *CSI: NY* flashed in my head, with me starring as the body!

I thought I better get out of there—fast, before this killer clown showed up. I was about to turn around, about to head back to my car, my mom's SUV parked on the road behind me . . .

But before I could, two lights flashed at me out of the darkness. Headlights. On for a moment. Then off.

There was another car parked on the Reservoir Road.

This didn't seem like a memory now at all. I didn't feel separated from my younger self. I felt I *was* my younger self again. I felt I was there, really there, really standing in the dark on the road, expecting to see the person who had killed Alex Hauser come leaping out at me at any moment.

I stood where I was, uncertain. Did I go toward the headlights and find out who had called me? Or did I do the smart thing and jump in my mom's car and drive out of there, tires squealing, just as fast as I possibly could?

I know, I know. The smart answer was obvious. I should never have gone out there in the first place. There could be no good reason to follow a mysterious voice into the darkness. There could be no good reason to stay here now that I'd come to my senses. I felt as if my heart were hammering in my throat—and that meant my body was trying to tell me something. It was trying to tell me: *Hey! Don't be an idiot! Go home where you belong!*

But I couldn't. What can I say? It was a guy thing. I knew I should never have come, but now that I was here—well, no way I was going to run for it. I didn't want to feel like a coward. I didn't want to let my dead friend Alex down. I wanted to finish what I'd started and find out who his killer was and be a hero, even if it got me killed. A guy thing, like I said. So no matter what the consequences, running away was just not an option.

Before I even came to a conscious decision, I was already moving along the road toward the place where I'd seen the headlights. With every step, my heart beat even faster. My body tensed as I tried to prepare myself mentally for any surprise attack. Soon, I could make out the shape of the car on the road ahead of me. It was a long black car of some kind: a limousine. Now I was close enough to see the silhouette of the man sitting behind the wheel. Was that him? I wondered. Was that the man who had killed Alex?

But as I took another step, the back door of the limousine came open. The light inside went on. I could see the driver was not alone. There was someone else sitting in the backseat.

I came around the side of the limo, closing the final distance to the rear door. The light inside was very dim. It didn't illuminate much. The driver's face was still in shadow—though I could make out a deadpan expression and cold, lidded eyes. And the man in the backseat was obscured by the top of the door frame. From where I was, I could only see him from the neck down, the suit and tie beneath his open overcoat.

I took another step toward the open door. Then I stopped. I bent down to get a look at the man's face. I didn't know him. He was older, fifty or something. A serious sort of person, a businessman or something like that.

"Get in, Charlie," he said. It was the voice I had heard over my cell phone.

I hesitated. Hadn't my mother been telling me since I was a child that I should never get in a car with a strange man?

The strange man in the car took out a wallet and flipped it open. I saw the government identification inside. I recognized the name of the agency. "Come on," he said. "We're not going to hurt you. We just want to talk."

Well, my mother always was a worrier. And I was a black belt, not a child anymore.

I took a breath and slipped into the limo's backseat. I pulled the door shut and turned to the man beside me.

"It's nice to meet you, Charlie," he said quietly. "My name is Waterman."

CHAPTER SEVEN

Out of the Past

Then I woke up. I was lying on the floor of the Panic Room. I was curled up on my side. The cot was right above me, as if I'd been lying on it and had fallen off. My clothes were damp with sweat. I smelled. And the room stank of puke.

I felt as though I had been lying there unconscious for a long time. I looked at my watch. I couldn't believe it. Almost ten hours had passed! It must be nearly morning now.

I started to uncurl. Bad idea. I was hit with a sharp

cramp in the stomach. I gave a growl and clutched at myself, curling up again, until the pain passed. Then, again—more slowly, more cautiously this time—I started to unwind my body. I rolled over.

The first thing I saw was the chair—the metal chair in the middle of the room. It stood above me, looming, threatening, frightening, the handcuffs dangling from the chair-arms, where they'd held my wrists.

I groaned and turned onto my back. The light from the fluorescents on the ceiling seemed to slice right through my eyes into my brain. Flinching, I raised a trembling hand to shield myself. With the other hand, I reached out blindly until I found the edge of the cot. Then I slowly pulled myself into a sitting position.

From there, climbing over the cot, I worked myself to my feet. For a moment, all I could do was stand there, swaying. The room seemed to turn and tumble this way and that. My stomach seemed to turn and tumble with it. I was light-headed. I was afraid I was going to throw up.

I moved to the steel toilet on the wall. That's where the smell of vomit was coming from. It made me feel even sicker. I reached out quickly and flushed the toilet, turning away so I wouldn't have to watch the swirl.

I moved to the middle of the room. I moved like an

old man, my legs stiff, my feet shuffling. I had to pause after a moment, resting my hand on the back of the chair to keep myself steady.

I felt like I had been run through a blender. For a minute or two, I was so dazed from the experience, I couldn't even really remember what had happened. Then it came back to me in flashes: the injection . . . the pain . . .

How much time had passed? I wondered. How long had I been in the chair? How long had I been lying on the floor?

The rest of it was coming back to me now too. The way I'd separated from myself, as if my soul had left my body. The way I'd stood on the sidelines and watched my own memories unfold . . . and the way I'd become one with the memory of myself standing in the dark on Reservoir Road . . . living through that walk to the car again and then . . .

I straightened. I whispered: "Waterman!"

I remembered now! That mysterious message on my computer monitor. The mysterious voice on my phone. Reservoir Road in the middle of the night. The mysterious black car. Waterman.

Even in my weakness and sickness, my mouth opened

and I let out a syllable of joy and hope. I gripped the back of the chair, holding myself steady. Yes—yes!—I was beginning to remember! I was beginning to remember it all. The days after Alex's murder. Beth and I falling in love. Then that message . . . that voice on the phone . . . that moment when I got in the car with Waterman . . .

I stood there, gripping the chair, fighting hard to remember what had happened next. I closed my eyes. I strained to see it. It seemed just out of reach, like a word you can't remember that's right on the tip of your tongue. I wanted so badly to get my memory back, to recall my life, but . . . No. Nothing. It just wasn't there. It hadn't come back to me. Not yet.

I opened my eyes. I looked down at the metal chair.

We're going to give you something that will make you remember, Waterman had told me. *I wish I could say it was going to be painless, but it's not. I wish I could say it was going to be instantaneous, but it's going to take time. Still, in the end, everything that has happened will come back to you.*

Everything, I thought. Everything will come back. That's all that mattered. I didn't care how much pain there was. I'd take the pain. I just wanted to remember my life.

Now my gaze lit on the steel chest standing against

one wall. There was a tray on the chest that hadn't been there before. There was a plastic bottle filled with water on the tray. There was a sandwich on a paper plate wrapped in plastic. I suddenly realized how thirsty I was.

I let go of the chair and moved unsteadily across the small Panic Room toward the chest. When I reached it, I saw there was a 3 x 5 index card lying between the water bottle and the sandwich. There was a note written in block letters on the card.

The note said: *Eat. Drink. Build up your strength. You're going to need it.*

There was no signature, just a doodled symbol, a hastily drawn stick-figure house—a square with a triangle roof on top and an X filling up the square.

I picked up the water bottle. It was one of those bottles with the built-in straws. I sipped at it gratefully. It was a shock when the cold water first hit my stomach, but then I felt the cold flooding through me, clearing my head, strengthening my body. I felt steadier almost at once.

I picked up the sandwich plate and carried it back to the metal chair. I unwrapped it. Turkey and cheese. I took a bite. It tasted good, but when it went down, there was a moment when I thought it would come right back up again. Then the moment passed, the food settled, my stomach settled. I felt hungry. I ate the rest of the sand-wich quickly, lifting the water bottle in between bites.

As my body felt stronger, as my mind cleared, I thought about what had happened. I tried to figure out my situation. Waterman had been honest with me. He'd said he was going to give me a drug that caused me pain and brought my memory back and that's what he'd done. It made me think maybe the rest of what he'd said might be true as well.

We're the good guys, Charlie. If liberty is better than slavery, like you said—if the people who work for liberty are the good guys—then we're the good guys, though we can't always be as good as we might like . . . We have to be sure you're still on our side . . .

The good guys . . .

As I took the last bite of the sandwich, I lifted my eyes to look at the wall, at the space on the wall where the secret door had been. I remembered more of what Waterman had said.

The Homelanders are close. Very close. They've hacked some of our files. We don't know how many. We don't know how much they know. But they know about me. They've been watching me for weeks. It's only a matter of time before they find this place and strike and try to kill us all . . . The people in this bunker are some of the only people left who can stop them. If they get to us, then we've got no chance.

I realized I had to talk to Waterman. If I couldn't remember what had happened with him in that car, then maybe he could explain it to me. In any case, I had to convince him that I was still on his side, that I was still one of the good guys, that if I could help him fight the Homelanders, I would do it, no matter what it took.

I set the paper plate down on the floor next to the water bottle. I stood up, my body stiff, but much stronger now. I moved to the space in the wall where the secret door was. I lifted my hand to knock . . .

Before I could, I was startled by a pounding that hit the wall from the other side. It was loud. It seemed to shake the room. It sounded as if someone was hammering his fist against the wall, just a little ways off to my left. I froze where I was, my hand lifted.

The pounding came again, moving now, coming toward me. *Boom, boom, boom.* As if the person was probing along the wall, trying to find an opening. Maybe trying to find the secret door into the Panic Room.

Who was it? Were they looking for me? Did they know I was here?

The pounding got closer and closer until finally it was directly opposite me. It was coming right through the wall across from me. Whoever was pounding was standing just a few inches from where I was standing with only the wall—and the invisible door—between us.

I stood frozen where I was. Waiting. Would he find me?

But the pounding continued moving along the wall. It went past me and on into the corner. There, finally, it ended.

All this time, I had stood rooted to the floor with my hand lifted, stopped in that moment when I'd been about to knock, about to call Waterman for help.

Now I lowered my hand. Whoever that was pounding on the wall, I felt pretty sure it wasn't Waterman.

Slowly, breaking free of my frozen surprise, I moved back to the wall. I pressed my ear against it. I listened.

The wall was thick. Very thick. The Panic Room had been built as a hiding place, not to be discovered. That made it hard to hear anything on the other side. There were voices—low, deep male voices—but I couldn't make out what they were saying. I pressed more tightly against the wall. I held my breath, straining to hear.

There was more conversation, dim, distant, wordless. I stood there, frustrated, unable to make out any of it.

Then an angry shout. For about two seconds, maybe three, the furious voice reached me clearly. It was a deep, hollow voice screaming in a language I didn't understand. Arabic, it sounded like.

The moment I heard it, the moment I heard that voice, my head snapped back away from the wall. A thrill of fear flared inside me. The voice faded from my hearing as I staggered back a step from the wall. I stared at the space. My mouth had gone dry. My legs felt weak.

I *remembered* that voice! Somehow, from somewhere. I knew the man who was speaking. I tried to picture his face, tried to call up his name, but I couldn't. It was just beyond the edge of my memory, a shadowy presence in the deeper darkness of the year I had forgotten.

Still—still—I knew him. I was sure of it. And I knew something else too: I knew he was a killer. Tough, vicious, wicked to the bone.

I could not recall his face or his name, but I knew this for certain: he was one of the Homelanders.

They were here.

CHAPTER EIGHT

Waylon

I stood there, frozen. I didn't even breathe. A thousand thoughts flashed through my head in a second.

Waterman's words: *The Homelanders are close. Very close . . . It's only a matter of time before they find this place and strike and try to kill us all.*

Had they done it? Had they broken in? Had they gotten Waterman and his friends? Or had he escaped? Where was he?

I knew I had to do something, had to move. It was like forcing myself to break free from a block of ice. But I did it. I made myself step forward, step back to the wall again. I made myself press my ear against the wall.

Once again, I heard that voice—now that I recognized it, I could distinguish it even though I couldn't hear the words. Again, the face of that vicious killer seemed to rise up out of the darkness of my memory—come close to the surface—then sink back down again into obscurity.

Then—startling—another shout—another voice—this one speaking English: "There's no one else in here either!"

The killer answered him with a shouted curse.

The other man shouted in English again: "There must be another way out."

Then a third man shouted: "Waylon! No one here either. Maybe they snuck him out before we showed up."

The killer—obviously their leader—shouted out another stream of Arabic.

I felt suddenly hollow inside. Hollow and weak and unsteady. I knew it was me they were looking for. And I knew that name too. The killer's name: Waylon. This was something I did remember clearly, something that had happened when I woke up strapped to that metal chair with the Homelander goons working me over.

There had been voices outside the door. There had

been a man with an American name but a thick accent: Waylon. He had been coming from the Homelanders' leader, a man who called himself Prince. He had given the order to my torturers:

The West boy is useless to us now. Kill him.

I understood why Waterman had put me inside the Panic Room. The Homelanders had been following him. They'd breached some of his files. They might know about this bunker. They might even have the entry codes. But he must've felt the Panic Room was still secure. He must've felt he could keep me safe here while I was help-less under the influence of the drug.

I listened. Outside in the main bunker, there was a pause, silence. I could feel them out there, on the other side of that wall. I could sense them looking for me, lis-tening for me. I felt that if I made even the slightest noise, they would hear it. They would find me. They would kill me. Waylon would finally kill me, as he'd wanted to do all this time.

Then, Waylon spoke. He was standing right next to me, directly on the other side of the wall. His voice seemed almost at my ear and, even through the thick wall, I heard every word he said with perfect clarity.

"All right. We'll have a look around for him outside

first. Then we blow this place to pieces. If he's hiding here anywhere, he won't survive."

One of the others answered him: "But I thought we were supposed to question him about . . ."

"I know what we're supposed to do!" Waylon shouted back. "But if he is here somewhere and we can't find him—we can't let him get away. Do what I tell you. Set the explosives! Make sure no one gets out of this hole alive!"

I heard them moving again, heard their wordless voices again, talking to one another, the sounds growing dimmer as they moved out of earshot, as they went to search for me in the ruins of the facility outside.

Then it was quiet.

I stepped back away from the wall again. I looked around. They were going to blow the bunker up. Just in case I was here. If they couldn't find me, they were going to make sure they killed me.

And now the Panic Room—the place Waterman had intended to be my refuge—had become my trap—and would be my coffin.

Because there was no way out.

CHAPTER NINE

The Second Wave

I stood where I was, turning this way and that, looking frantically around me as if I might discover some other exit.

But there was none. I knew there was none. The only entrance and exit was that secret door, and I didn't know the code that opened it. That code—that series of passes Waterman had made with his hand to make the door slide open: I had tried to follow it, to memorize its straight lines and slashes, but it was way too complicated to fix in my mind. I had only the vaguest idea of the pattern.

I stepped up to the wall. I passed my hand over it. It was an act of pure desperation. I tried to imitate the straight lines and diagonals Waterman had made. But of course nothing happened. The door didn't open. It was hopeless. I was stuck in here. Stuck while the Homelanders prepared to blow the place—and me—into oblivion.

I looked around again, hoping for another idea. I saw the chest. I moved to it quickly. I knelt down beside it. I took the tray off and placed it on the floor. Then I pushed up the lid of the chest. It opened easily.

There was a pile of blankets inside. I pulled them out quickly, tossing them onto the floor. There was nothing underneath. The chest was empty. I felt the bottom, some crazy idea forming in my head that maybe there was a trapdoor, a secret tunnel or something like that. No such luck.

I crouched back on my heels and tried to think. There had to be something I could do. There had to be something I could at least try.

An idea began to form in my mind—and as it did, a slight hope began to rise in me . . .

And then, suddenly, out of nowhere, the pain struck again—that writhing, fiery snake of pain that I'd felt when the crow-faced woman injected me. I cried out and twisted backward, as if I could escape it. But it gripped me from within, twisted me, made me thrash helplessly on the floor for an endless second, and then another, and then . . .

It all began again. I felt myself break free of my body, as if my soul were floating away. I could see myself there below, twisting on the floor, gripping my stomach, but I couldn't feel the pain anymore. My body grew more and more distant. I reached out for it, trying to grab hold of myself, to get back into myself. I couldn't leave my body now! This was no time to go flying into the past—not with the Homelanders getting ready to dynamite the bunker.

But there was nothing I could do. I couldn't stop it. I drifted further and further away until even the urgency of my situation seemed part of another world, another life. A moment later, I had forgotten what the urgency was. I was entering an all-surrounding darkness, turning away from my lost body, turning toward a small point of light that I knew contained my memories . . .

In a flash, I was there, in the past. I was in the long black limousine. I was sitting in the backseat with Waterman. I wasn't watching the scene this time. I was in it. I was part of it. I was living it again.

The black limousine was moving now. It had left the

reservoir behind. The driver was guiding it into the darkness of the hills around my town. There was nothing on either side of us but looming forest and the night.

"What I'm about to tell you is a secret," Waterman was telling me. "A secret of the United States government. If you tell anyone, you'll be endangering people's lives. I want to know if you're ready to hear it and if you can promise me not to tell anyone, not even your parents, not even your closest friends, no one."

I sat in the darkness, nervous. Was this guy really an intelligence agent for the United States government? What did they have to do with what happened to Alex? What did they have to do with me?

"Okay," I said. "I promise not to tell. What's the big secret?"

"We want to frame you for Alex's murder."

I sat staring at him as if I hadn't heard him. I hadn't really—at least I hadn't been able to totally comprehend what he said. The meaning of it reached me slowly. And then I answered, "I . . . What?"

"We want to plant your DNA on the murder weapon, traces of Alex's blood on your clothes. We want to rush the case to trial as quickly as we can and basically railroad you into prison for murder."

I went on staring at him—or at his shadow in the dark. It seemed to take long, long minutes before each new sentence he spoke made sense to me. "You want to send me to prison?"

"Oh, don't worry, we're going to help you escape."

"Oh."

"But your family, your friends, your girl, everyone you know, is going to think you're a murderer—and you won't be able to tell them the truth."

I didn't answer. There was no answer I could think of. What could I say? I sat there, nodding. "Whoa," I said finally. "You want to frame me for murder, put me in prison, and make everyone I know think I'm a criminal. That's a really great offer. Is there a second choice? Like: you shoot me in the kneecap and leave me by the side of the road to die?"

Waterman gave a small snort of laughter in the dark. "Doesn't sound like much fun, does it?"

"Any," I said. "It doesn't sound like *any* fun. But since you have the word *intelligence* in your agency, I'm guessing you have some reason for wanting me to do all this."

"We do," said Waterman. I heard him take a deep breath, as if he needed strength before he tried to explain this to me. "Your friend Alex was murdered by one of your teachers at school."

"What?" I blurted out. Immediately, my mind went through a roster of my teachers. I couldn't think of any one of them who would murder somebody. Okay, maybe Mrs. Truxell, the girl's PE instructor . . . but no, not really, not even her. "Who?" I asked. "Who killed Alex?"

"Mr. Sherman. Your history teacher."

"No! Come on!"

Waterman shrugged in the shadows.

"That's ridiculous," I said. "Sherman's an idiot, but he's not a killer."

"Actually, I'm afraid you've got that backward, Charlie. He's a killer, but he's no idiot."

I brought my hands to my face, confused. For a moment I felt that I was forgetting something important . . .

And then, I was in the dark again, looking through a sort of keyhole of light, looking in at my own body where it lay writhing in agony on the floor of the Panic Room.

They're going to blow it up! They're going to blow me *up! I've got to get back there! I've got to stop it! I've got to get out of this flashback!*

For that one moment, I remembered my present situation, my present danger.

But the next second, as if I'd reached the end of some enormous elastic tether, I was snapped backward out of consciousness and hurled into the past again . . .

Back onto the seat of the dark limousine next to Waterman.

"Your history teacher is a member of an organization that's dedicated to attacking this country in any way it can," he was saying. "They call themselves the Homelanders. The group was begun by Islamo-fascists in the Middle East, but they've come here to recruit Americans who don't like the way our country works and who want to join with them in fighting us."

"Sherman . . . ?" I shook my head. Sherman and I had had our disagreements over the years, big disagreements about freedom and the founding ideals of our country—the stuff you talk about in history class. He always made fun of me in class, in fact, for being a patriot, for believing in the words of our Declaration of Independence that people are "created equal," and "endowed by their Creator with certain unalienable rights," like life, liberty, and the pursuit of happiness. Sherman didn't believe in any Creator, for one thing, so he didn't think there was anyone to endow us with rights. And he thought leaving people free to pursue their own ideas of happiness led to too much selfishness and unfairness in the world.

"Look," I said, "I never agreed with Sherman about much, but I always figured it's a free country, he's entitled to his opinions."

"He *is* entitled to his opinions," Waterman said. "In fact, as far as I'm concerned, the Islamo-fascists are entitled to their opinions too. They're just not entitled to force their opinions on the rest of us, or to kill and terrorize people who disagree with them. And Sherman's not entitled to drive a knife into the chest of a seventeen-year-old boy because he decided he didn't want to join with the Homelanders after all."

"Alex?" I said. It was almost too much to take in. Not almost—it *was* too much to take in. "Alex was going to join them?"

"Sherman convinced Alex that he could somehow solve his personal problems by joining the Homelanders. And that was Alex's plan until that night he talked to you. I don't know what you said to him exactly, but we think it caused him to have second thoughts—and Sherman killed him to keep him from revealing the Homelanders' existence—and maybe to protect himself from the consequences of his mistake in bringing Alex on board. The

Homelanders aren't that nice to people who make mistakes."

I shook my head again, trying to get my mind to come to grips with this. "So Alex was going to join the terrorists, only then he didn't, so Sherman killed him . . ."

"That's it."

"So you want to frame me for murder? I mean, where does that come in?"

Waterman shifted in his seat, turning to face me. "We think, if we play this just right, we can get you into the organization."

"What? Me? You want me to become one of these Homelander terrorist guys?"

"As things stand, we could just arrest Sherman for murder. We might even be able to make a case against him. We might be able to pressure him into telling us what he knows. But the fact is, we already know what he knows—and it isn't all that much. He's been kept out of the centers of power and information because he hasn't earned the trust of the high command. Losing Alex hasn't helped his reputation with them either. That's why he'd be eager to recruit someone like you . . ."

In spite of my shock at hearing all this, I actually

laughed out loud. "Recruit me? To the Homelanders? Big fat hairy chance, man. Sherman knows better than to think he can recruit me to attack this country. I think this country is one of the best ideas human beings ever had . . ."

"Well, I think you're right about that, Charlie. But I think you're wrong about Sherman. In his efforts to please his masters, he's been arguing that you're the perfect recruit."

"The per—Me? But . . . why?"

"Well, you're a fighter, for one thing. And for another, you're kind of the all-American boy, you know? With a face like yours, you can get in anywhere. And on top of that . . . well, Sherman's theory is that you're a true believer. Because you're patriotic and religious, he figures you're the type of person who follows along blindly, without thinking. He figures all he has to do is replace your patriotism and your faith in God with *his* beliefs and you'll be willing to follow after him."

"But that's crazy! I don't just believe in anything that comes along. I've thought a lot about the things I believe. It's about people being free and . . ."

Waterman raised a hand. "You don't have to explain it to me, son. We know all about your beliefs, Charlie.

Your beliefs are exactly what we're counting on. I'm just talking about what Sherman thinks. We feel if we can set up a scenario where it seems you have reason to feel bitter and disgruntled—like your being unfairly convicted of murder, for instance—it'll give Sherman fresh motivation to approach you and win you over. And it'll make your conversion believable to the people in charge."

"Okay," I said uncertainly. "I get that, I guess. So I'm unfairly convicted and Sherman recruits me. Then what?"

"Then you work your way into the organization. You go through their training, you get assigned to carry out a terrorist attack and find out about any other attacks that are being planned. Then you help us prevent the attacks and find the people in charge so we can bring them to justice."

When Waterman was done, I sat in silence. I guess you could say I was dumbfounded. I mean, listen, I would do just about anything to protect this country, its freedom, its people. I already wanted to join the Air Force, and protect it from the sky. But this . . .

"Why can't you just use one of your own people?" I said after a while. "I mean, you're spies, right? This is what you do."

"We've tried that. The Homelanders are too good,

too sharp. We believe they even have people with access to government records. They see through our cover stories, they spot our agents. But someone like you. A teenager. Someone with no connection to us . . ."

"Yeah, I get it, I get it."

"That's why there'll only be a small number of people—just me and a few others in the organization and one other outsider—who'll know what's going on, who'll be able to prove your true purpose and identity."

I shook my head as the whole picture finally made itself clear to me. I turned away. I stared out the window of the limousine.

"Look, you don't have to give me an answer now," Waterman went on. "And before you do answer, I want you to understand completely what I'm asking of you. You'll be taken away from your family, your school, your friends, your girlfriend. They'll all believe you were convicted of murder. They'll believe you're a fugitive who's escaped from prison. They may even come to learn you've become a member of a group of terrorists. I can't say how long it will be before you can come home and tell them the truth. It might take a month, six months, a year—I just don't know. In the end, if you succeed, if you infiltrate the Homelanders, if you bring these people down before they can attack us, maybe you'll be a hero. Maybe they'll give you a parade in your hometown. But if you get caught, if the Homelanders expose you, kill you . . . Well, what we're doing isn't exactly legal, doesn't exactly have the approval of all our higher-ups, you understand me? If it all goes wrong, we'll never admit we know you, we'll never tell anyone the truth. Everyone who loves you will go to his grave believing you betrayed your country."

I went on staring out the window. I didn't see the forest passing or the sky above the forest or the stars gleaming in the sky. I didn't even see my own faint reflection on the window glass. All I could think of was the people I knew. My mom and dad. Beth. My friends at school. All I could see was the look in their eyes—what that look would be when they saw me accused of murder, when they saw me convicted, taken off to prison. I mean, my mom—she worried frantically about me even at the best of times. I couldn't take a walk without her thinking I was going to trip and fall down and break my leg or something. How would she ever get through something like this? How would she ever be able to stand it?

But on the other hand . . . on the other hand, if what this Waterman guy was saying was true, if there really

were people who wanted to attack this country, to terrorize people, to bring down all the things that had made us,
really, the freest nation that had ever existed in all the
long history of the world . . . then how could I just stand
by and let it happen? How could I say no?

I turned back to Waterman . . .

And in a snapping flash of light, the scene was gone.
I was gone. There was nothing but a sort of woozy, searing darkness and then . . .

I opened my eyes. I was on the floor of the Panic
Room, my cheek against the cold tiles. For a moment I
couldn't think of anything, couldn't remember where I
was or what was happening.

And then I did remember. I remembered the limousine. The forest passing outside the window. Waterman.

We want to frame you for murder.

I sat up quickly. I winced as a dagger of pain went
through my head, and a wave of nausea washed through
my stomach. But I gritted my teeth and fought the pain
and sickness down. What did it matter? A little pain
was nothing. A little nausea—nothing. I remembered! I
remembered what had happened. I remembered how I
had become part of the Homelanders.

I was working for Waterman, for America. I was

infiltrating the terrorist organization in an effort to bring them down.

My hands curled into tight fists. My vision blurred with emotion. I remembered! What I'd done, who I was. All the people who believed in me—my parents, Beth, my friends, Sensei Mike—all the people who *hadn't* thought I was a murderer after all, who had trusted I wasn't one of the bad guys even when I'd doubted it myself. They'd all been right. I'd never hurt Alex, I'd never been a terrorist, I'd only broken out of prison as part of the plan . . .

For a second, all I could do was sit there, staring through the blur of emotions, joyful and grateful to God that my life was finally coming back to me.

And then—then my mind cleared. My vision cleared. I looked around and saw where I was. I remembered what was happening.

I was in the Panic Room. Stuck here behind a door I didn't know how to open. Stuck here while the seconds ticked away and the Homelanders prepared to blow the place to smithereens.

CHAPTER TEN

The Sign

Fighting off my headache and my stomachache and the weakness in my muscles, I grabbed hold of the side of the chest and pulled myself to my feet. How long had I been out? I looked at my watch. I'd only been unconscious about twenty minutes this time. It wasn't much, but it was long enough for the Homelanders to have set a bomb and run for it. The explosion could go off any minute, any second, for all I knew. How much time did I have left?

I stared at the wall in front of me—the wall that held the invisible door—that blank, blank wall. The Panic

Room struck me as a good name for this place just then because I could feel myself starting to panic.

But then, as my mind continued clearing, something came back to me. What was it? Just before that last seizure—the last "memory attack," you might call it—I'd had an idea, hadn't I? An idea had started to take shape in my mind about how I might be able to get out of here—maybe even get out before the killer—Waylon—and the rest of the Homelanders blew the place up.

What was it? What had I been thinking?

I looked around, trying to recapture the half-formed thought. My gaze fell on the chest, the empty chest. Something . . . Something had been there . . .

And then I saw the tray. The tray that had had the sandwich on it. I'd taken it off the chest when I'd opened it. I'd set it on the floor . . . There was something about the tray, something on the tray . . .

It all came back to me.

A flash of pain went through my forehead as I reached down and picked up the 3 x 5 index card Waterman had left for me with the food and water. I had to shut my eyes a moment until the headache passed. But a moment later, I forced my eyes open. I reread the message written on the card:

Eat. Drink. Build up your strength. You're going to need it.

And then, at the bottom, that symbol instead of a signature: that simple stick-figure house, a square with an X inside and a triangle for the roof.

Why would Waterman sign the note that way? That was the thought that had come to me just before the memory attack knocked me down. What did the symbol mean? The answer had been coming to me when the seizure hit and drove me to the floor and back into the past.

It occurred to me that he must've been trying to tell me something. Why else sign with a symbol instead of his name? And *what* else could he have been trying to tell me except how to get out of here?

I remembered how I'd watched him passing his hand over the secret doors. I remembered the pattern had been all straight lines and diagonals. Just like the little house— the straight lines of the walls, the diagonals of the roof and the X inside. Waterman must've been passing me the code just in case—just in case the Homelanders arrived— just in case he had to escape and couldn't help me.

That's why he didn't explain it. Why he didn't write it out. He was afraid they might be watching, maybe even afraid they had someone inside his organization. I didn't know. But since that little house symbol was the only hope I had—the only idea I had—I figured I better try to do something with it—now, before Waylon's bomb went off.

I moved to the wall again. I was about to put my hand against it, when I hesitated. I pressed my ear against the wall instead. I didn't want to get out of here only to walk directly into the guns of the Homelanders. I listened. There were no voices out there now, no one talking. The place was empty—or it sounded as if it was empty anyway.

I backed off. I put my palm on the wall, the way I'd seen Waterman do it. I traced the shape of the house. The square base. The X inside. The triangle of the roof.

Nothing. No motor noise. No sliding door.

I licked my dry lips. My heart was sinking. I could almost feel the seconds ticking away. I tried again. Again, nothing. Maybe the door had some kind of secret sensor that read Waterman's fingerprints or his DNA or something.

But then why leave me the symbol?

I thought back to when I'd seen Waterman make the sign over the door. I could see there was a pattern. It was always the same pattern—the lines and diagonals. But there was something else as well. He had always done it in one smooth, flowing motion, never breaking off, never moving his hand and never retracing any of the motions he'd already made.

There must be a way to draw the little house with the X inside in one motion without lifting my hand from the wall.

I tried it. No, I had to go over one line twice. I tried it again. Then again. I couldn't make it happen. Every time, I had to retrace one of the lines. And every time I was done, there was no motor. No door.

I stared at the pattern on the card. There had to be a way. Waterman did it. I could do it. He wouldn't have given me the symbol if it didn't work. I had to believe that or there was no hope.

I tried again. I traced a diagonal across the wall. Another one. Another. Wait, this time it was working. A straight line, drawing the house. Then—yes!—only one more line. I did it. I finished the whole thing without retracing my steps.

And immediately, there it was. The grinding engine in the wall. The panel slid back in front of me.

The door to the Panic Room was open. I was free.

I stepped out into the main part of the bunker—and the first thing I saw was the bomb.

It was sitting in plain sight, right there on one of the workstations. It was a large cube made of several blocks of some kind of brown putty. Explosives. I'd seen stuff like that on TV. There was a device and wires wrapped around the putty block. There was a timer there with red numbers quickly blinking away.

Six minutes and fifteen seconds left before the bomb exploded; 6:14 . . . 6:13 . . . The numbers clicked swiftly down.

That was the first thing I saw. The next thing I saw was the Homelanders.

A movement caught my eye. I turned toward it. Something was moving on one of the monitors hanging on the wall. It must have been displaying the video read-out from a security camera posted in the ruins above.

I could see by the video that the dawn was breaking outside now. There was a clear view on the monitor of some of the broken pillars and ruined buildings standing in the morning mist. I could see the Homelanders moving among them. Searching through them.

They were searching, I knew, for me.

I turned from monitor to monitor. Each one showed

a different portion of the scene outside. Each one showed different ruined buildings, different columns and empty arches and patches of fog snaking through them, twining around them. Each monitor also showed one of the Homelanders.

I counted six of them altogether. Each one carried a machine gun. They moved slowly through the ruins, their heads turning this way and that, their eyes scanning the area.

All except one. One stood still. He held his gun with its butt propped on his hip, the barrel pointed to the sky. I recognized the place where he was standing. He was right outside the brick cylinder that protected the entry. He was guarding the only way out of here. He was making sure I didn't escape.

So down here, the bomb was ticking—six minutes and one second now . . . 6:00 . . . 5:59 . . . 5:58 . . .

And up there, the Homelanders were patrolling and guarding the way out.

If I stayed in the bunker, I'd be blown up. If I tried to leave, I'd be shot.

I looked at the bomb on the table again. For a moment I wondered if maybe I could just disconnect the wires and defuse it. But somewhere in the bottom of my mind was the absolute certainty that the device was sensitive to the touch. Maybe it was something I knew from my training with the Homelanders. But however I knew it, I felt very sure if I even touched the device, it would go off then and there.

So that was what I saw: first the bomb . . . then the Homelanders on the monitors patrolling the ruins outside . . . And then . . .

Then I turned to look around the room, to search for another way out or for a tool or weapon I could use in a fight—and I saw something else.

On the threshold of the doorway into the next room, there was a puddle of blood.

The breath came out of me with a trembling "Oh!" I had a terrible feeling I knew what I would see if I went into that room.

But I had to go. I had to see. I had to know what was there.

I started moving. As I came closer, I saw a trail of blood leading away from the puddle, leading into the other room.

And then I came closer and I saw a hand—one outstretched hand lying on the floor.

And I came closer. Closer to the door. I saw the arm

attached to the hand. I reached the doorway and looked in.

That's when I saw the body.

It was Waterman.

He was lying on his face in the middle of the floor of a room that looked like a small lounge. One arm was tucked under his torso. The other was outstretched, the hand pointing to the doorway through which I'd just come. Beneath his head, there was another pool of blood.

I rushed to him. I knelt beside him. I felt his neck for a pulse. There was none.

He was dead.

CHAPTER ELEVEN

Time Running Out

The world seemed to spin around me. I thought the jolt was going to overwhelm me. Waterman dead. Executed by the Homelanders while I lay unconscious and undiscovered in the Panic Room.

And all the others? Gone. Escaped? Dead? I didn't know.

I stood up and staggered back to the door. I leaned heavily against the frame.

Waterman was dead. My contact. My ally. The only ally whose name I knew. Even if I managed to get out of this death trap alive, where would I go now? Who would I turn to for help?

A wave of hopelessness washed over me. I felt as if all my strength had drained away. For a second or two, I actually thought I wouldn't be able to move again.

But there was no time for that. No time to indulge that sort of emotion. The bomb was ticking. I had to keep going, had to. Waterman was dead. All right. That's the way it was. He had died trying to protect America from its enemies—trying to protect liberty from its enemies. A lot of people have died that way in a lot of places over the years. God knows their names—every one of them—I believe that—but they're beyond my help. The only thing I could do was go on, never give in, keep fighting the fight they fought.

I pushed off the door. I forced down my dizziness and sickness. I felt something flaring up inside me, a new heat, a new fire of determination. I knew I had only minutes to live. But I was going to use every one of them. I was going to do everything I could to get out of here, to find help, to find someone who would believe me when I told them about the Homelanders, to find someone who would help me stop them, help me bring them down.

A new bolt of pain went through my head, and for a

second I was afraid another memory attack would knock me over. I couldn't let that happen. I massaged my brow with my fingers, trying to think. My eyes went to Waterman's body one more time. The pool of blood. The outstretched hand . . . I wondered . . .

As much as he could, Waterman had tried to watch out for me, to think of me and my safety. He had brought me to this bunker in the hopes of evading the Homelanders. He had hidden me in the Panic Room so I wouldn't be discovered during the memory attacks. He had left me the symbol so I could escape if he was captured or killed. And now . . .

I looked at the pool of blood on the floor. The trail of blood leading into the room. The second pool beneath Waterman's head.

He had been shot in the doorway. He had struggled to get into the room. He had managed to position himself before he was shot again—position himself with his hand outstretched, pointing . . .

I turned and followed the direction of Waterman's hand. He was pointing to the slim section of wall beside the doorway. That's all it was, a slim section of wall between the door and a metal shelf. Blank wall.

I went to it. I raised my palm. I traced the shape of

the house against the blank wall. Instantly, there was the sound of a motor. A panel slid back. A small panel this time. A hidden cache about the size of a paperback book.

I reached into the cache and at once my hand touched a metal object. My fingers closed over it. I drew it out.

I knew what it was as soon as I saw it. It was the little gizmo Milton One had been holding when I first came into the compound. The little control panel the size and shape of an iPhone. It was the thing Milton One had used to control Milton Two, that flying security robot that had blasted me when I tried to escape from Waterman and Dodger Jim.

I looked from the little device back to Waterman's body where it lay on the floor.

"Thanks," I whispered to him.

The Homelanders had killed him—and now they were trying to kill me, to make sure there was no one left who could stop them.

Well, they could try. But at least now I had a weapon. Waterman had left me a weapon.

And I wasn't going down without a fight.

CHAPTER TWELVE

The Battle Begins

Four minutes thirty-three seconds . . . 4:32 . . . 4:31 . . .

I was glad to get out of that room of death. But the moment I moved back to the main part of the bunker, I saw the bomb again and the seconds ticking away. I stood in front of the device, holding the small controller to Milton Two in my hand. Four minutes twenty-five seconds now . . . So little time.

I tore my eyes away from the red numbers and looked down to study the controller.

At first, the little screen was blank. But I found a

button built into the top of the device and pressed it. The gizmo's monitor light came on. The small screen showed a terrain map with a green dot blinking on it and several blinking red dots as well. There was also a series of numbers up in the right-hand corner. More than anything, it reminded me of a PSP video-game screen.

Which was a good thing. I was always a pretty decent gamer. Not a game-dork or anything: I didn't sit around getting fat on Pop-Tarts while fragging Covenant Grunts for fourteen hours at a time or anything. But when a cool new game came out, whether it was an old-fashioned platformer or a full-blown shooter, I was usually the first among my friends to get the hang of it. For some reason, I had a knack for figuring out a level even while escaping a horde of zombies through an underground storage facility. My dad sometimes said kind of bitterly that my generation had developed some new sort of DNA that helped us understand games—but I think he was just jealous because he usually got killed while he was still lifting up his eyeglasses in order to see which button on the controller was which.

So, forcing myself to stay calm, to ignore the dwindling red numbers on the time bomb, I did a quick study of the controller's readout.

I could see right away that the terrain on the screen was the terrain outside: the trees were dark green patches and the buildings were shapes outlined in red. The green dot—that was probably M-2 himself. The red dots were probably bio-heat readings—the Homelanders. There was no way to identify what the numbers were, but I was guessing they were probably M-2's speed, height, blast energy, and number of tear-gas shots—something like that.

I glanced up. I couldn't help myself. The timer was ratcheting rapidly down to 4:00.

Come on, I told myself, *concentrate*.

I looked down at the controller again.

According to my reading of the map, Milton Two was lying on the ground at the very edge of the ruined compound outside. When I tilted the controller, the green light stopped blinking and the numbers changed: M-2 was rising off the ground and taking flight. I quickly found I could move him by either tilting the device or touching the screen. And more. The moment he started moving, a small square window lit up in one corner of the screen. It was video—the point of view from the camera in M-2's single eye: it showed what M-2 saw in front of him. There were also two red buttons that lit up on the

bottom of the controller. The one on the right was to fire electronic blasts. The one on the left let loose tear gas.

Again, I couldn't stop myself from looking up at the clock: 3:56 . . . 3:55 . . . 3:54 . . . I seemed to feel every second dying inside me as it ticked away.

I glanced over at the monitors on the wall. I could see the Homelanders there. Three of them had stopped moving now. They had taken up positions, standing with their guns propped on their hips. They were guarding the area, waiting for the explosion that would destroy the bunker—and me, if I was still inside.

Okay, I thought. *Okay*. I needed a plan of attack. What would give me my best chance at getting out of here?

My first thought was to send M-2 after the guy near the entrance in the brick cylinder. I remembered the pain of getting hit with M-2's blaster: it paralyzed me, knocked me right off my feet. If I took out the entrance guard, maybe I could break out and make a run for it. But then I thought: *No*. Once the blasting started, the others would be alert. They'd come running in the direction of the fight. If I hit the entrance guard, they'd converge on the doorway, closing off my escape.

So the best idea was to strike *away* from the entrance

...irst and hope the guard outside the brick cylinder abandoned his post so I could get away.

I studied the wall monitors quickly. All the Homelanders were at their positions now. They were communicating with one another through microphones clipped to the shoulders of their khaki jackets. The leader—the killer I knew as Waylon—was posted off at the perimeter, about as far from Milton Two as he could be. Waylon, I could see now, was a big man, tall and broad shouldered, with heavy, sagging features and a scruffy black beard. He had deep-set eyes that were always moving, watchful. I doubted M-2 could cross the facility and reach him before he or one of the other Homelanders spotted him and possibly shot him down.

I looked at another monitor where another man was standing beside a broken column of stone. This guy was young—maybe my age. Tall and skinny with light blond hair and a long, narrow face. His eyes looked angry and mean. I looked down at his feet. The morning mist curled around his hiking boots. But as the mist moved and cleared in patches, I could make out Milton Two—the little device shaped like an Xbox controller—lying in the grass about twenty feet away from him. Then the mist closed again and M-2 disappeared behind it.

I looked at the ticking clock on the bomb.

3:00 . . . 2:59 . . . 2:58 . . .

There was no more time to think this over. I had to attack.

I tilted the controller. Reading the altitude numbers—looking up at the monitor—looking at M-2's point-of-view screen, I could keep my little electronic pal low to the ground, hidden in the mist. I tilted the controller forward and M-2 began to fly at that low altitude, brushing through the grass as he approached the knees of the blond Homelander standing guard nearby.

M-2 moved silently. The blond Homelander didn't hear him coming. But if I was going to get a good shot, I was going to have to come up higher. I tilted the controller forward. The numbers ratcheted up as M-2 lifted into the air, up around eye level. Now I could see the blond guard's face in M-2's POV screen.

I glanced over at the monitor. The blond guy still didn't see M-2 coming.

Just a few more feet.

I stole a glance at the clock: 2:30 . . . 2:29 . . . 2:28 . . .

Then: "Hey!"

I nearly jumped out of my sneakers. The voice had come directly from the controller in my hand. I looked. I could see the blond guard in M-2's POV screen. He had sensed M-2 approaching. He had turned. He had seen the little device flying through the air straight at him and had cried out, his voice caught on M-2's microphone.

Now the blond guard pulled his machine gun off his hip. He was turning around to face M-2.

I pressed the Fire button.

The electronic blast shook the controller in my hand—just like the vibrating function in the Xbox controller. The flash of electricity hit the blond guard smack in the forehead. He gave a cry and went tumbling backward, the machine gun flying out of his hands. Then he was down—and M-2 was still hovering near the place where he'd fallen.

But now I saw on the controller map: the red dots were on the move. I could hear voices—shouts—coming through the controller's speakers. Not only that: I could see by the readout that M-2's blast had depleted his energy and the numbers were low—though they were already climbing back up as he recharged his blaster from his energy source.

I glanced up at the monitor. Waylon was barking orders into his shoulder mike. The other Homelanders were charging toward the place where the blond guard had fallen. They were bringing their guns to bear on M-2.

All of them, that is, except the guard at the bunker exit. He had lowered his machine gun and was standing at the ready, but he stuck to his position, blocking my route of escape.

The three other guards converged on M-2. I had to keep him moving or they'd blow him out of the sky.

I looked at the clock on the bomb.

2:20 . . . 2:19 . . . 2:18 . . .

The Homelanders kept closing in on M-2. The clock kept ticking down.

2:17 . . . 2:16 . . .

Two-minute warning.

I had to get out of here. Now.

CHAPTER THIRTEEN

Race for the Trees

I looked down at the controller. The red dots continued closing in on the green dot. Now they were near enough so I could see the guards advancing in M-2's POV screen as well. Grim, determined faces getting closer and closer. Guns raised, pointed right at my little flying ally.

I held the controller steady. I let M-2 hover there in the air. The clock on the bomb approached two minutes. The three charging Homelanders steadied their machine guns as they charged toward M-2.

I tilted the controller, wiggling it left and right at the

same time. M-2 flew straight at his attackers, ducking this way and that as he came.

The three Homelanders opened fire, blasting away with their machine guns. The noise of it reached me distantly through the controller's tiny speaker. I saw the coughing flame from the barrels in the POV screen.

But M-2 was a small target, moving fast and dodging back and forth—up and down now too. He got closer to them without getting hit. Closer, zipping and zigzagging through the hail of bullets.

And now, I heard the Homelanders cry out, cursing in frustration as M-2 zipped right into the midst of them, making it impossible for them to shoot at him without killing one another. One of them swiped at the flying device with the butt of his gun, trying to knock it out of the sky. It was a near-miss, but I cocked the controller and M-2 levitated above the swinging gun.

Then I pressed the button to release the tear gas.

Instantly the view through the POV screen went foggy white as the gas was released. I saw the Homelander guards for another second. I saw them clutching their throats. I saw their tongues coming out as they started gagging and coughing. Then they reeled back every which way, stumbling off into the smoke, where they vanished.

Now M-2 and I were both moving at once. I started for the bunker exit, working the controller even as I went. I guided M-2 through the smoke, out into the open air. I found the red dot standing outside the cylinder—the guard just outside the bunker entrance.

M-2 flew at him. I flew at the door.

Now I was standing in front of the wall. I worked the controller clumsily with my left hand as I raised my right hand against the place where the hidden door was. I glanced down at the controller, tilting it this way and that to keep M-2 flying at the guard by the brick cylinder. Now I could see the guard on the POV screen: a short, thick-necked bull of a guy with dark skin and bright, wicked eyes. He had his gun at the ready and was staring in confusion at his friends where they reeled and choked in the tear gas. I could tell by the look on his face that he hadn't spotted M-2 coming at him yet. Those bright eyes of his were scanning the sky, searching for the flying security device.

I tilted the controller and sent M-2 right at him.

Then I turned to the door. With my free hand, I quickly traced the lines and diagonals on the wall. I had a moment of panicky doubt: What if it didn't work? What if the code was different for this door than it was for the door of the Panic Room?

But no. The engine made its grinding noise. The panel slid back. I stepped out into the dark antechamber at the bottom of the cylinder's steps.

And then—gunfire.

I was so startled, I nearly dropped the controller. I froze where I was at the foot of the stairs. The sound had come from the speaker in the device and from the outside world above me at the same time. The thickset guard at the entrance was firing at M-2, his teeth bared as he moved his machine gun back and forth and sent a wild spray of machine-gun bullets at the zigzagging thing that was racing toward him.

I could feel the time bomb ticking off its last two minutes in the bunker behind me. But I had to stop where I was. I had to pay attention to what was happening on the controller's screen.

I could see the barrel of the guard's machine gun flashing as M-2 raced toward him. Once again, I worked the controller to keep my little ally moving back and forth, up and down, dodging the spray of bullets as they came.

Then the gunfire stopped. I heard the fat guard give a curse. He was out of bullets. I saw him on the POV screen as he hurled his machine gun to the ground, reached inside his khaki jacket and pulled out a pistol. He started to lift it, started to point it at M-2. I saw the black darkness of the bore.

But he was too late. M-2 was in range now. His blaster was fully recharged. I fired and hit the fat guard square in the chest. I saw his face contort in pain as the shock went through him. Then he was gone, collapsing like a tower of blocks when you pull out the bottom one.

I'd done it. He was down. I grabbed hold of the banister and started up the long flight.

I took the stairs two and then three at a time, going as fast as I could to get away from the explosion that I knew must now be only a minute and a half away.

Now I was on the landing. Now I was making the sign of the house again in front of the blank wall. Now the engine was grinding, the door was sliding back.

I used the moment to glance down at M-2's controller.

I saw Waylon's face, contorted with rage, filling the POV screen as he rushed toward the entrance, toward me.

The door kept sliding open, revealing the fat guard where he lay on the threshold, unconscious. In another second, I'd be exposed, giving Waylon a clear shot at me, an easy chance to blow me away. At the same time, though

M-2's blaster was still recharging, it wasn't anywhere near full power yet.

Now the door was half open. I looked up. There was Waylon. Our eyes met and a thrill of terror went through me as I remembered his cold, amused voice giving the order to kill me.

He saw me too. He lifted his machine gun, pointing the bore at my chest.

And there was M-2 as well. I saw the little device hovering in the air just beside the onrushing Waylon.

Quickly, I glanced down at the controller and pressed the Fire button.

I looked up in time to see what happened next right in front of me outside the open door.

M-2 let out a weak blast, using all the power he had left. It hit Waylon in the side of the head. The terrorist leader cursed, losing hold of his gun as he gripped reflexively at the wounded spot. The gun was strapped around his shoulder so he didn't drop it, but it swung loose as he staggered to the side, dazed.

It was my moment—my only moment. I leapt over the fat guard and ran for it.

I dashed out of the brick cylinder and into the ruins of the old hospital complex. The forest mist surrounded me as I ran past crumbling columns and empty buildings with shattered windows that stared like eyes. I saw the three guards where they stood trying to recover from the tear-gas blast. I saw the fourth guard—the blond guy M-2 had knocked over with a shock—trying to sit up. Then I lost sight of all of them as I ran behind a freestanding wall. Up ahead, I saw the woods. If I could get into the trees, I thought, maybe I could lose myself in the forest.

But just then: the stuttering cough of machine-gun fire. Dirt flew up at my feet as bullets dug into the earth.

I leapt to the side and rolled. There was a crumbling column of stone. I got behind it before the shooter found his range. The bullets struck the column, throwing chips of rock into the air.

Lying breathless on the ground behind the column, I looked down at the controller still gripped in my hand. When I tilted M-2 toward the nearest red dot, I saw Waylon in the POV screen. He'd recovered from the half blast and was coming after me, machine gun lowered, ready to open fire again when he had me in sight. If I broke from behind the column, he'd mow me down easily.

M-2's blaster charge was still too low to get off another shot. But I thought maybe I could use the tear gas again to put Waylon out of commission. Hiding there behind the column, I tipped the controller and sent the security device flying after him even as Waylon came charging toward me.

Waylon came closer to the column. M-2 came closer to Waylon. I put my finger on the firing button, ready to unleash the gas.

But before I could, Waylon suddenly stopped in his tracks. He wheeled toward M-2. My flying pal was moving too fast to stop. He was too close to get out of the way. I peeked out from behind the column. I knew what was going to happen a second before Waylon pulled the trigger.

Waylon fired and M-2 exploded in a sparking, sizzling white and red flash. I felt my little friend die in the rattle of the controller in my hand.

But there was no time to mourn for plastic and wires when so much flesh and blood were at stake. Waylon's back was turned to me as he shot M-2 out of the air. I seized the opportunity. I bolted from behind the column, hurling the useless controller away as I ran.

The ruin of a large, warehouse-like building stood in the mist off to my right. I ran for it, hoping to reach cover before Waylon could turn and find me. I was almost there when he opened fire. My heart seized with terror at that deadly, rattling sound. A bullet ricocheted off the wall of the building just ahead of me. I threw up my arms to protect my face as I was hit by flying shards of plaster.

Then I was there, dodging behind the same wall, out of the range of the stream of bullets.

I raced along beside the building. If I could reach the far side before Waylon came around behind me, I might have a chance of breaking around the corner for cover and then dashing all the way into the trees.

I ran full tilt, my face contorted with the effort, barely aware of my own exhaustion and breathlessness. All I could think was that any second Waylon might clear the corner behind me and pump a stream of machine-gun bullets into my spine.

I was nearly there. Running. Nearly there.

And then two guards stepped out in front of me, blocking my way.

CHAPTER FOURTEEN

Zero

It was two of the guards I'd hit with tear gas. A moment later, the third one joined them. Then the fourth—the lanky blond guy M-2 had laid out with his blaster. All four of them blocked my way with machine guns lifted directly at me.

There was nowhere to go. No way to escape without being turned into Swiss cheese. I pulled up short. I saw the Homelanders' fingers tighten on the triggers of their weapons. I thought they were going to shoot me dead then and there.

"Put your hands up!"

The voice came from behind me. I looked around and saw Waylon at my back. He had his machine gun trained on me too.

"Put 'em up!" he shouted again.

I raised my hands over my head. I turned to face him.

He stalked toward me angrily. I expected him to pull the trigger any second. But he kept coming until he was standing mere inches away from me, his furious eyes peering into mine. He stood like that a long second, his teeth bared. Then . . .

"Pig!" he said, and he slapped me.

It was a hard shot with the back of his hand. It landed full force to the side of the face, nearly knocking me over. I fell two steps to the side, my face stinging, my head feeling thick, my vision blurred.

Before I could recover, Waylon grabbed me by the front of my fleece and swung me around, hurling me against the side of the building. I gave a loud "Oof!" as the impact knocked the wind out of me. Waylon gripped the fleece harder, twisting it back so that his fist pushed into my throat, cutting off my air. He leaned in close to me as I struggled for breath.

"I ought to kill you right where you stand," he said in his thick guttural accent. "And I will kill you, that's a promise. I will kill you just as surely as I killed your friend in the bunker."

"Waylon . . . ," said one of the other guards, a husky man with a big handlebar mustache.

"Shut up!" Waylon shouted—and the handlebar guy did as he was told.

Waylon's face was close to mine. His fist dug into my throat. He grinned as I gasped and choked. Something stirred in my mind, some memory of him linked with fear. I didn't know who Waylon was—I still couldn't recover his image from wherever it was hidden in my brain—but it was there, all right, somewhere, and the memory was associated with terror.

"But before I kill you, we're going to have a talk," he told me. "We're going to finish the conversation we started before you ran away. And this time, there's not going to be any escape. This time, you're going to tell me everything."

"Waylon . . . ," said the handlebar guy again.

Waylon ignored him. He was enjoying himself too much. He was enjoying his threats, enjoying the fear he must've seen in my eyes, enjoying my fight for breath as he twisted his fist into my throat.

But even as his threats and his rank breath washed over me, I understood what the handlebar guy was trying to tell him, I understood what was going to happen next, and I was getting ready for it.

"There's no one left to help you," Waylon said. "All of Waterman's friends have run off like the cowards they are. There's only one other person who knows about you at all. And before you die—which will be in agony, by the way—you're going to tell me who he is, and you're going to die knowing that I'm going to kill him too. Because we're almost ready to—"

And then the bunker blew up underneath us.

The time on the bomb had finally winked down to zero. The explosives went off and the blast was tremendous. Everything in that bunker—including Waterman's body—must have been blown to smithereens.

And it rocked the ground above as well. It shook under my feet like an earthquake had hit. The four guards staggered—but they'd been waiting for it—waiting and trying to warn Waylon that it was coming. But Waylon hadn't listened. He'd been so completely distracted by his dealings with me that the noise and the rumble took him totally by surprise.

His eyes went wide and he lost his grip on me,

instinctively grabbing his gun to keep it secure as he stumbled a step to the side. It was only a step. He was about to recover.

But before he could, I punched him.

It was a full-force uppercut. I'd been ready to throw it, waiting for the chance. And, to be perfectly honest, it had a little extra charge in it because, for some reason, I just didn't much like this guy. My fist connected with his jaw. He would've gone flying backward if I hadn't grabbed hold of his arm with my left hand at the same time. Quickly, I twisted him around and wrapped my arm around his throat, holding him in front of me, between me and the other guards. I took hold of his gun and twisted it upward, jamming the barrel under his chin.

The four guards had recovered from the force of the blast and had their guns leveled at me, but they froze when they saw me using Waylon as a shield.

"Stay where you are," I told them. "I don't want to kill him, but I will."

And I would've too.

Waylon was still heavy in my grasp, nearly unconscious from the uppercut to his chin. He was woozy and staggering. Only by using all my strength could I keep him in place in front of me.

"You got nowhere to go, West," the blond guard growled at me furiously.

But I was already backing away from him, backing away from all of them, edging toward the trees that surrounded the ruins.

"West!" the blond guard shouted in his fury and frustration.

I kept going, backing away, holding Waylon up in front of me, holding his gun up under his chin. As I came to the edge of the ruins, there was some sort of structure standing there in the morning mist: the slanted ruin of a wall, I guess, with rebar sticking out here and there from the concrete.

I slipped behind the structure, out of range of the guns of the other four guards.

Just then, Waylon started to come around, started to struggle in my grip. I slammed him into the concrete. He grunted. And while I had him pressed dazed against the wall, I stripped the machine gun off his shoulder.

I backed away from him, the gun leveled at him.

He turned slowly. His dark face looked lopsided as it swelled in the place where I'd slugged him. His eyes were bright—nearly white it seemed with the light of the hatred burning in them.

"Where do you think you'll go?" he snarled at me. "The police want you. Your own people don't know you. You can only bring danger to your friends. Even if you get away, I will hunt you down, so help me."

"Then maybe I ought to kill you here and now," I said.

Waylon laughed. "But you won't."

I didn't answer. I knew he was right about that. There was no way I was going to pull the trigger on an unarmed man.

Now the other guards were coming into sight, moving around to get a bead on me around the side of the wall.

"Call them off," I said to Waylon. "Tell them to lower their guns. I won't kill you if I can help it, but if they start shooting, I start shooting—and you're the first to go. They can't kill me quick enough to stop it."

Waylon glanced to the left and right where the guards were spreading out to surround me. I could see he didn't want to give the order. But I could also see he didn't want to die.

"Lower your guns," he shouted—barely able to get the words out through his clenched teeth. "Lower them."

I glanced at the guards. They were still aiming at me.

"Do it!" I shouted. "Do it now or I'll kill him!"

One by one, the Homelanders pointed their machine guns at the ground.

I started backing away from Waylon, backing away from the ruins, backing into the mist that gathered where the forest began.

Rubbing the side of his face where I'd punched him, working his jaw against the pain, Waylon kept his angry eyes on me.

"I'll be seeing you, West," he said.

I didn't answer. I was pretty sure he was right. We weren't finished with each other.

I felt a chill as I stepped into the deeper shade of the trees, as the forest mist closed around me. It was the chill of the damp and cold, but it was a chill of fear as well.

With one last glance at the Homelanders standing there, I turned and sprinted into the trees as fast as I could.

CHAPTER FIFTEEN

The End of the Chase

I heard Waylon's furious shout behind me: "Go after him!"

I looked back over my shoulder as I ran. I saw the guards coming into the woods, hunting for me. But they were moving slowly. Wary, watchful. I had a gun now, and they knew I could turn around any minute and open fire on them if they just charged blindly ahead. They were scanning the trees, pushing branches and brush out of their way to make sure the path was clear before stepping forward.

I, on the other hand, ran full speed. I cut like a deer through the mist and shade, dodging under branches, leaping over roots and stones, flashing in and out of sudden patches of sunlight and large areas of deeper darkness, trying to put as much distance between myself and my pursuers as I could.

When I looked back again, I couldn't see them. I couldn't see anything but the tangle of trees and forest vines. I stopped. I leaned the machine gun against a tree. I bent over, my hands on my knees. I was gasping, trying to catch my breath. For a moment or two, my panting was the only sound I could hear.

Finally, when I could, I breathed more softly. I listened. Yes, I could still hear the Homelanders. I could hear their footsteps crunching on the forest duff. I could hear them calling to one another in the trees.

"You see him?"

"No."

"Wait. Here's a trail. He went this way."

They were tracking me, following the places where I'd broken through branches and brush or turned over leaves. They were coming on slowly, but they were coming on steadily all the same. Their voices sounded closer every minute.

I had to keep going, but I was tired. The agony of Waterman's memory medicine . . . being trapped in the Panic Room . . . my escape from the bunker before it blew up . . . my tangle with Waylon and the guards . . . and then my run through the woods—all of it had worn me out. My legs felt weak. My energy was depleted. I knew I couldn't keep running like this forever.

I straightened and looked around. These woods were deep. No sign of an exit. Without a firm sense of my direction, I might find myself circling around in them until nightfall. I knew there had to be a road here somewhere, but I had no clue where it was. I needed a place to hide, a place I could rest and gather my strength and get my bearings.

By listening to the voices and movements of the oncoming Homelanders, I could pretty much judge their location. I could tell they had spread out in a line—like a search party—in order to comb through the forest more efficiently. Instead of running away from them, I now began traveling across that line, hoping to get outside the reach of it. I had gone only a little ways when I found something—maybe just the hiding place I was looking for.

I came to a small stream. A little ways beyond it, a steep formation of rock and earth rose about thirty feet into the air. Its gray and brownish color blended with the gray and brownish colors of the surrounding forest—the naked winter trees and the dirt. I hadn't even known the formation was there until I was practically right beneath it. I thought: *If I could get up on top of that, the Homelanders might pass right under me without even looking up. If they did look up and spot me, at least I could fight them from high ground.*

I paused at the stream, laid my gun aside, and knelt down to drink. The water was gritty and had a sour, coppery taste, but man oh man, I was grateful for the coolness of it in my hot, dry mouth, grateful for the sense of fresh strength flowing through me. When I'd had my fill, I stood up. I strapped the machine gun over my shoulder again. I stepped across the stream and attacked the rock.

It wasn't an easy climb. It was hard to find places to grab hold of. I dug my fingers into the moist earth between the rocks. I dug the toes of my sneakers in wherever I could. My arms and legs felt weak, but once I was six feet off the ground, there was no turning back, and no letting go. I climbed hand over hand until the slope grew a little less steep. Then I scrambled the last several yards to the top.

Here, there was an outcropping of gray rock. I edged

out onto it and lay down on my stomach. Now I had a good view of the forest below me.

The morning was wearing on. The mist was thinning. Sunlight had begun to pierce through the needles of the high pines and the empty branches of the winter maples. It fell in beams with the mist swirling inside them. The shadowy tangles of the forest depths came into sharper relief as the light grew stronger.

And there were the Homelanders. I could see four of them in a long, straggling line, moving slowly through the trees, their machine guns strapped to their shoulders and held at their sides. I could hear them talking to one another across the small distances between them, just the sound of their voices at first and then, as they got closer, their words.

"He was running fast. He must've gotten pretty far by now."

"He's gotta give out eventually. He can't just keep going and going."

"I don't know. He's a tough kid. Lot of determination."

"He gave Waylon a pop, that's for sure."

"Yeah, you don't see that too often."

"Well . . . Waylon will take it out of him when we finally catch him."

They came closer and closer. I got out of sight, lying low on the outcropping, pressing my face to the cold of the stone, feeling the cold of the mist swirling over me. Now, the gunmen's voices were practically right underneath me. When I peeked over the edge of the outcropping, I could clearly make out the faces of the two men nearest me.

"I tried to warn Waylon that explosion was coming . . ." It was the guard with the handlebar mustache, shaking his head ruefully as he scanned the woods. "Dude wouldn't listen."

The blond guard answered him with a nasty laugh. "Well, man, you should tell him that. You should just say to him, 'Waylon, dude, I tried to warn you, but you were just too stupid to hear what I was saying.'"

The handlebar guy gave a heavy laugh in return. "Right, I should do that," he said. "Because my life just won't be complete until I have a bullet in my kneecap."

They passed on, right by me. They never even looked up at the rock where I was lying. Soon, their voices were fading into the woods to my left. For now, at least, I was safe.

Weary, I rolled over onto my back. I stared up into the thinning mist that clung close to my face. With the danger having temporarily passed, all the emotions of the last several hours washed over me. It wasn't a good feeling.

You got nowhere to go, West.

Blond Guy was right about that, wasn't he? For so long, it seemed, one idea had inspired me and kept me from giving up hope.

You're a better man than you know. Find Waterman.

Ever since that moment when I'd been arrested, when the police had been leading me to the patrol car to take me off to prison . . . ever since that moment when someone had somehow unlocked my cuffs and whispered those words in my ear, my one hope had been that I might find Waterman, that he might tell me the truth about what had happened to me.

Well, I'd found him, all right. And with the help of that drug the crow-faced woman had injected into my arm, I was beginning to remember the missing year of my life, beginning to get at that truth I'd wanted so badly. The reason I'd been convicted of Alex's murder . . . the way I'd fallen in with the Homelanders . . . I hadn't remembered all the details yet, but I could pretty well guess what they were. And Beth . . . my love for Beth . . . I knew it was there all along, but I'd forgotten it. How desperate I'd been to get that memory back again—and now I had.

But what good did any of it do me? Waterman was dead. All his compatriots had vanished. If there was anyone left who could prove I wasn't really a killer, I didn't know who it was or where he was. Detective Rose and the rest of the police were still trying to arrest me for murder. The Homelanders were hot on my trail, guns at the ready. I still couldn't go home, couldn't go to my parents without putting them in danger. I couldn't go to see Beth. What good was the memory of loving her now?

I stared up into the mist, and I felt totally alone. I tried to pray. I did pray. At least I said the words, asking for guidance, asking for help. But my heart wasn't in it. I could feel myself holding back somehow, keeping my distance from God.

Somewhere in the Bible—I couldn't remember where just then—it says you're supposed to be happy about the hard things that happen to you, you're supposed to be grateful for the "trials" you go through because they test your faith and harden your endurance. Well, I definitely wasn't happy—or grateful. The truth is: I was angry, ticked off to the maximum. I was sick of trials, sick of being tested. I was eighteen, for crying out loud. I was supposed to be getting ready for college. I was supposed to be with my girl. I was supposed to be preparing for life.

It wasn't fair that things should be so hard for me, so dangerous. It wasn't fair that there was no one to help me, that God wouldn't help me, that I was all alone. I wanted my life back, my ordinary life. I wanted to go home. It wasn't fair.

What am I supposed to do now? I asked God bitterly, thinking about that horrible scene in the bunker lounge, Waterman lying there in a pool of blood, dead. No one left to help me. No one left who knew I was innocent. *What am I supposed to do now?*

And the answer came back to me:

You got nowhere to go, West.

I let out a long, slow sigh. I rolled over and pushed up to my knees. I looked off into the woods and could just make out the four Homelander guards disappearing among the trees. The tendrils of mist curled around their vanishing figures. The sunlight fell in beams behind them, lighting patches of the forest floor.

Exhausted, heartsore, I moved to the edge of the rock and went down until it became too steep to keep walking. Then, I slipped over the side. Digging my fingers into the outcropping, I reached down with my feet until I found some purchase in the earth and stone. I began the climb back to the forest floor.

Well, I thought, *at least I'm safe for now. I suppose that's something. I suppose I ought to be grateful for that.*

And just then—just as I thought that—I felt the pain flaring inside me again—that pain brought on by the drug Waterman had given me.

I had time to think, *Oh, no! Not now!*

And then the attack came full force, the writhing flame of agony twisting inside me.

Crying out, I lost my hold on the rock. Suddenly, I was falling, falling, falling into darkness and memory.

CHAPTER SIXTEEN

The Choice

It was different this time. I had nothing like that feeling I'd had before that I was leaving my body. I was just suddenly somewhere else. I wasn't even aware that it was a memory. I was completely *there*—completely present in the past without any idea that I had fallen from the rock, that I was lying on the forest floor now, writhing in pain . . .

I was in school. I was sitting at my desk in English class. Mrs. Smith was in front of the room, sitting on the edge of her desk holding a book. Mrs. Smith was one of

my favorite teachers. She was a young woman with a very happy, upbeat personality, always smiling and joking and laughing with the students. She was a little on the round side, but I thought she was pretty all the same, with long blond hair and sort of an open face that always looked pleasantly surprised.

She was reading from the book in her soft voice—a play by William Shakespeare: "'Between the acting of a dreadful thing / And the first motion, all the interim is / Like a phantasma, or a hideous dream . . .'"

The kids in the class—including my friends Josh and Miler—sat around me at their desks, listening. Most of them—including Josh and Miler—looked pretty bored.

My desk was near the window. I turned away from Mrs. Smith and the others and looked out at the school grounds. There was a square of open grass surrounded by low buildings. It was lunch hour for the younger kids, and I could see some of them out on the kickball field and others studying at outdoor picnic tables and some just sitting together and talking, joking around. I watched them sadly.

Have you ever had to get through a day, smiling at people, talking, as if everything were normal and okay, while all the time you felt like you were carrying a leaden weight of unhappiness inside you? That's what it was like for me. I had been at this school now for three years. Before that, I had been at middle school for two years with most of the same kids. And before that, most of us had been together at elementary school. I could stroll across this campus from one end to the other and never be out of sight of a familiar face.

This school, these people, this town—this was my life, my whole life. Sure, I always knew I'd leave it someday. I always figured there'd be college. I had a secret hope that maybe I could get into the Air Force, be a fighter pilot. I knew there'd come a time when life would take me other places.

But what was happening now, this was different. It was terrifying. And it was hugely sad.

I want you to understand completely what I'm asking of you. You'll be taken away from your family, your school, your friends, your girlfriend. They'll all believe you were convicted of murder. They'll believe you're a fugitive who's escaped from prison. They may even come to learn you've become a member of a group of terrorists . . . If it all goes wrong, we'll never admit we know you, we'll never tell anyone the truth. Everyone who loves you will go to his grave believing you betrayed your country.

That's what Waterman had said to me that first night we'd driven around the hills in his limousine.

Since then, there had been other nights. Waterman and I had met by the reservoir again and again. He and his driver—the man I came to know as Dodger Jim—had driven me to what they called a safe house: a cabin hidden in the woods. Waterman had shown me videos there on a laptop, videos of the Homelanders. As I watched the vids, he explained who they were, what they'd done.

He'd shown me their leader, who called himself Prince. He was a Saudi Arabian terrorist who'd blown up buildings in Britain and Israel. In Tel Aviv, he'd planted a bomb in a school, killing twenty-seven little children. Now he was here, recruiting Americans to act as his proxies in his war against the West and against our liberty.

Then there was one of Prince's top lieutenants. He called himself Waylon. He was an Iranian. He'd helped kill American and British soldiers in Iraq. When he was finished there, he'd gone after civilian targets, kidnapping and killing journalists and Western aid workers in Afghanistan. He liked to torture people and kill them slowly and then send the videos to their families. Waterman showed me some of those pictures too.

And he showed me other things. Snapshots of Waylon meeting with Mr. Sherman, my history teacher. Intercepted e-mails in which Sherman told Waylon about how he was recruiting my friend Alex to join their team . . .

These were the people who had come to America to fight against us. Every night we met he showed me more videos, gave me more of their literature to read, literature full of hatred—hatred of Americans, Britons, and Jews—hatred of liberty, which they called a tool of the devil—hatred of anyone who disagreed with or opposed them.

And every night we met, Waterman asked me again: Would I join with him in fighting them? Would I give up my home, my friends, my girl, my life to try to stop them?

Now here I was, back in school on what was supposed to be an ordinary day, trying to pretend that everything was normal, while those words of his weighed on me and turned everything into suspense and sadness:

If it all goes wrong, we'll never admit we know you, we'll never tell anyone the truth. Everyone who loves you will go to his grave believing you betrayed your country.

"'The Genius and the mortal instruments / Are then in council,'" Mrs. Smith read on. "'And the state of man,

/ Like to a little kingdom, suffers then / The nature of an insurrection.'"

Right, I thought. That was me: my mind and my heart fighting with each other. Or my "genius" and my "mortal instruments." Or, like, whatever. The point is, I didn't know what to do.

I looked at Mrs. Smith and I felt a lump in my throat as if any moment I might just break down crying. How could I say yes to Waterman and just let this life of mine disappear, break the hearts of the people who loved me, say good-bye, maybe forever, to my parents, my lifelong friends, the people I loved?

And Beth . . .

The bell rang.

Mrs. Smith snapped the book shut. "Read this scene again at home and we'll talk about it tomorrow," she said.

I just sat there, not moving, staring at her, wondering if I'd even be here tomorrow, wondering if I'd ever be here—or see any of these people—again.

"Hey! Ho! I know it's poetry, man—but wake up." It was Josh, slapping at my shoulder. I looked up at him. Josh was kind of a geek—kind of the Ur-Geek, actually— the Geek on whom all other geeks were modeled: short, narrow with hunched-up shoulders. Short curly hair and thick glasses and a nervous smile. "It's time for some of us to have lunch and others of us to gaze stupidly into our girlfriend's eyes while little heart-shaped bubbles come blipping out of our ears and nostrils."

"You make it sound so romantic," said Miler Miles beside him. "Or maybe *disgusting* is the word I want." Miler was a track star: small, lean, with short blond hair and green, go-get-'em CEO-of-the-future eyes.

I went on sitting there, just sort of gazing up at them stupidly. My buddies. They'd been snarking like this at each other for years now. Josh's geekiness could push the needle on the annoying meter into the red sometimes, but he was really smart and we all liked him anyway. And Miler—he was just a regular guy now, but he practically had "I will be a gazillionaire businessman one day" flashing in big lights over his head.

What would it be like never to see them again? Not just because we'd gone off to college where we could communicate online and meet up on vacations and so on. But never to see your best friends again at all? Or talk to them at all? Or even be able to tell them the truth about yourself? To tell them you weren't the bad guy you were supposed to be?

Everyone who loves you will go to his grave believing you betrayed your country.

"Uh, hello? Earth to Starship Charlie," Josh said.

I blinked. I realized I'd been sitting there staring at them. I tried to think of something funny to say—something that sounded normal. "Oh, sorry. What you were saying was so interesting I guess I dozed off."

It was lame, but it was the best I could come up with. I gathered my books and shoved them into my backpack. Slung the backpack over my arm as I got up and joined Josh and Miler.

"It's hard to communicate when you're wrapped in a cloud of looooove," said Josh, singing the last word as if it were opera.

"Or maybe it's just hard to communicate with a member of a subhuman species who can't get within ten feet of a girl without melting into a pile of quivering mucus," Miler said.

"How can you tell when Josh melts into a pile of quivering mucus?" I asked. "I mean, what's the difference?"

"Good question," said Miler.

"Har har," said Josh, but he smiled nervously because—well, because he always smiled nervously.

Miler and I bumped fists and laughed. My heart felt as if it were made of lead.

The three of us walked outside into the crisp, cool air.

We strolled together across the grass toward the cafe-teria, nodding or waving every three steps or so at someone we knew.

I heard Waterman speaking again: *We want to rush the case to trial as quickly as we can and basically railroad you into prison for murder.*

Prison, I thought. What would it be like to be in prison for murder? Would they be able to protect me from the *real* murderers all around me or would I be on my own? I could just imagine my mother coming to see me on visiting day . . .

"You all right?" said Miler.

I blinked at him, coming out of my thoughts. "What?"

"You just groaned. Are you sick or something?"

"Oh . . . no, I was just . . . I just remembered I forgot to study for my calculus quiz," I lied.

"No big deal. You didn't want to go to college anyway. You can always work at Burger Prince. Of course, if you want to move up to Burger *King*, you will need a BA."

As we reached the door of the cafeteria, there was a burst of laughter and we nearly bumped into three people coming outside. It was two younger students—and Mr. Sherman. They'd obviously been joking about something together.

"Hey, guys, how's it going?" said Mr. Sherman, slapping Miler on the shoulder.

Josh and Miler said it was going okay, but all I could do was stand there and stare. Mr. Sherman was a youthful-looking guy, trim and fit with a friendly smile. I'd had him for history two years in a row. Was it really possible he was the one who stabbed Alex Hauser in the chest? Was it possible he was a member of a group dedicated to terrorizing and killing Americans?

"What's the matter, Charlie?" he said with a grin. "You look like you've seen a ghost."

"No . . . hey, Mr. Sherman . . . ," I answered quickly, but my voice trailed off. I couldn't think of anything to say.

Sherman gave me kind of a strange look—but then he was moving off across the quad, followed by his two students. I heard the sound of their laughter fading as they moved away.

I was still watching them go as Josh, Miler, and I stepped into the cafeteria.

I'd never really thought much about the cafeteria before. You don't, you know. It's just the cafeteria. You go there, you eat your lunch, so what? But now, it struck me—how familiar it was. How reliable the smells of it were.

Hamburgers Monday, mac-'n'-cheese on Wednesday . . .
The food was—well, it was no better than it is at anybody
else's school cafeteria and we were always making jokes
about it—like,

How can you tell the difference between rubber and a
Spring Hill High hamburger?

You can swallow rubber.

And the colored plastic chairs were uncomfortable
and there were all kinds of annoying high school social
rituals like this kid won't sit with that kid, and the popular girls always sit over there and giggle about the
popular guys, and the sad-sack guys always sit over
there and make snarky jokes about the popular girls,
and so on . . .

But it's strange about this stuff. When you might be
about to lose something forever, you begin to think about
it in a different way. This cafeteria—with its so-so food
and uncomfortable chairs and all the general social stu-
pidity that could keep you awake nights if you thought
about it too long—this cafeteria had been a huge part of
my life. We'd had some big laughs in this place—me and
Josh and Miler and Rick. Like the time Josh was telling
some stupid story and gesturing wildly with his milk carton and the milk flew out and hit Mr. Cummings smack

in the face. And we'd had some big drama here too, like the time I faced down Mike Hurtleman because he'd dumped Owen Parker in the garbage can headfirst. This is where I was sitting at lunch one day not too long ago when Beth first came up to me, when I first worked up the courage to ask her if I could call her and she wrote her phone number down on my arm . . .

I mean, look, I don't mean to get all sentimental about it. It was just the school cafeteria. I didn't want to marry it or anything. But what would it be like when I was eating my meals in a cafeteria in prison and instead of sitting with people who dump kids in garbage cans or write phone numbers on your arm, I was surrounded by guys who would happily cut your throat?

"Dude!"

I blinked. I looked at Miler. "What?"

"It's just a calculus quiz," he said.

"What do you mean?"

"You groaned again."

"Oh . . . forget it," I told him. "I'm just . . ." But I didn't know what I was just doing.

"Anyway," Josh chimed in, "there's the steamy-dreamy love of your vaguely embarrassing life."

I blinked again and saw Beth waving to me from a

table across the room. She was there with Mindy and Jen, a couple of her friends.

"So if you sit with the girls," Josh said, "does that, like, make you a girl too?"

"Go on," said Miler. "Have fun. If you need me, I'll be over here trying to explain to Josh what girls *are*."

I was walking across the cafeteria toward Beth when suddenly I had the weirdest experience. It was almost like a hallucination. I had this powerful, powerful sense that I wasn't here in the cafeteria at all, that I was somewhere else, in the woods somewhere, lying on my side in a pile of leaves, twisting on the ground in pain and trying to pull myself out of it because there were bad men hunting me, because I had to keep running, keep trying to escape . . .

I shook my head and the vision was gone. I thought: *That was weird. All this emotion and indecision must be starting to get to me.* Then I continued walking across the room to Beth.

"Aren't you going to get anything to eat?" she asked as I sat down across from her.

I muttered something about how I'd had a snack earlier. The truth was, with that lump in my throat, I didn't think I could eat anything. I didn't *want* to eat anything.

I just wanted to sit there. I just wanted to look at her. I just wanted to be with her. Because I might never have a chance to be with her again.

I sat down. Mindy and Jen started talking to each other, obviously trying to give Beth and me some time for conversation. I tried to think of something to say, something ordinary and cheerful. But my voice kept trailing off, and I guess I kept sitting there for long seconds just kind of gazing at Beth.

"Are you okay?" Beth asked me.

And I said, "Yeah. Yeah. I'm fine. I'm just . . ." And then my voice trailed off again.

And then, just like that, I thought to myself: *I'm not going to do it. I mean, I don't have to do it. No one can make me do it. All I have to do is say no and Waterman goes away, right? The whole thing goes away just like that. They can find someone else to frame for murder. They can send someone else to prison to have his throat cut. Someone else's mother can sit on the other side of the prison glass, sobbing. Let someone else leave his life and his friends and his girlfriend behind forever. It's probably all baloney anyway. I mean, Sherman—a terrorist murderer? No way. Maybe this Waterman is just some nutcase who goes around pretending to work for the government . . .*

As I went on thinking these things, the sadness began to lift from me. It really was as if someone had taken this huge boulder off my back. I began to feel practically lighthearted. Why had I been torturing myself like this? Just because some guy named Waterman showed up and proposed this insane plan didn't mean I had to agree to it. It wasn't written in stone or anything. All I had to do was say no, and the whole thing would go away.

I reached out across the table and Beth reached out and we held hands. A surge of feeling for her went through me. It wasn't the first time I'd felt certain she had been created especially for me, that we had been created especially to find each other and be together.

This is good, I thought. *This is what really matters in life. I'm not giving this up for anyone.*

And with that, my sadness was gone completely. I was happy, in fact. In fact, I felt great.

Suddenly, in the blink of an eye, I was in the karate dojo. For a second, I felt confused. How had I gotten here? Wasn't I in the forest somewhere . . . ? lying on my side writhing in pain . . . ? people searching for me . . . ?

No. No, now I remembered. I was back in Spring Hill. I'd gone home after school. I did my homework. I borrowed my mom's car to drive to my karate lesson . . .

Now I and my sometime-karate-partner Peter Williams were moving together back and forth across the dojo carpeting. We were doing a paired *kata*, a kind of mock fight where I would move through one memorized series of punches and blocks and he would go through a complementary series so that every time I punched, he deflected it and struck back and then I deflected his punch and struck back and so on.

Sensei Mike moved along beside us, watching us, calling out instructions: "That foot should be right between his feet, Charlie. You're not close enough. You can't reach him with that punch. Come on, pay attention, West; you know better than that."

I was making a lot of mistakes. I knew the material really well and I was trying to keep up, but my mind just kept going back to my next planned meeting with Waterman—tonight. I kept thinking: *I'll just tell him no, that's all. All I have to do is say no and things'll be back to normal.*

But at the same time I was also thinking about my friend Alex. Stabbed in the chest, dying in the park, whispering my name with his final breaths. What if it really had been Sherman who'd killed him? What if he really was part of a terrorist organization out to attack America?

How could things ever go back to being normal now that I'd heard what Waterman had to say? Once you know something, you can't un-know it.

"All right, chuckleheads, that's enough," said Sensei Mike. "Williams, bow out and hit the changing room. West, stay here and tell me what's on your mind and why you're messing up so badly—and it better be something really, really important—like your shoes are on fire or something."

"No, no, it's nothing, Mike," I muttered. I didn't like to lie to him, but I'd promised Waterman I wouldn't tell anyone what he'd said. Government secret and all that. I stood there in my karate *gi*, my head down. I was still breathing hard from the exercise. "I'm just . . . distracted, that's all."

"Uh-huh," said Mike. I could tell he didn't believe me. Mike had this amazing ability to figure out pretty much everything that was on your mind just by watching your karate practice.

For a second, I stood there, not really knowing what to say, not wanting to lie any more than I had to, unable to tell the truth. Then, the words sort of just came out of me: "Hey, Mike, can I ask you a question?"

"No. And don't ever try it again."

I rolled my eyes.

Mike pulled his mustache down over his mouth with one hand, hiding a smile. "Go ahead, chucklehead. What question?"

I hesitated. Mike never talked much about being in the Army or what he did in the War on Terror. He never told anyone how the president gave him a medal for running to an armored truck under fire, getting hold of a big .50-caliber gun, and fighting off more than a hundred Taliban to save his fellow soldiers. He never told anyone about getting hit by a bullet that day and having to have a piece of titanium put in his leg where the bone used to be. But I'd looked him up on the Internet and found out all about it.

"You know that thing you did in Afghanistan? That thing you won the medal for from the president?" I asked him.

Mike's hand went on hovering at his mustache. He did that a lot, usually to hide his smile. Mike always had this smile on his lips and this look in his eyes like he was secretly laughing at something. It was as if he thought just about everything was a joke, as if the whole world was just one big collection of chuckleheads making a mess of things and it was all pretty funny. But now, his eyes had gone serious. The smile that usually hid behind his mustache was gone.

"Yeah," he said quietly. "Yeah, I seem to remember something about that."

I wasn't sure I should go on. I knew he didn't like talking about it. But now that I'd started, I said, "Would you do it again? Knowing you could get killed. Knowing you might never get home to see your wife and daughter. Now that you've had time to think about it, I mean, away from the battle, if you could go back and make the choice sort of more, I don't know, calmly . . . would you still do it?"

For a long moment, Sensei Mike didn't answer me. The dojo was quiet except for the sound of Pete banging around in the changing room in back.

When he did speak, Mike still didn't answer me. He just said, "Life's funny, chucklehead. You only get one and you don't want to throw it away. But you can't really live it at all unless you're willing to give it up for the things you love. If you're not at least *willing* to die for something—something that really matters—in the end you die for nothing."

Then, all at once, I was standing in the dark. I looked around me, dazed. Where was I? Oh yes, now I saw. I was at the reservoir again. Back at the place where I always met Waterman. There was my mom's SUV parked by the curb . . .

Tonight was the night. I was going to give Waterman my answer. I was going to make my choice.

I had that weird feeling of confusion again. How had I gotten here? Hadn't I just been in the dojo a second ago? But no, now it came back to me. After talking to Sensei Mike, I'd driven out to the end of Oak Street. I'd parked in the same place I'd parked that night Alex and I had our argument, that night he'd gotten out of my car and walked into the park where he was killed. I'd sat there behind the wheel of my mom's SUV and stared through the windshield into the twilight descending on the park. I prayed silently. I asked God to help me figure out what I should do.

As always, the prayer helped. As I stood out by the reservoir now, I *did* have a clearer idea of what I was supposed to do. The only problem was: I didn't want to do it. I didn't even want to think about doing it. I just wanted to tell Waterman no—no, thanks. I want to live my life. I want to go to college. I want to join the Air Force. And hey—by the way, I just fell in love. I mean, do you mind? Couldn't you just leave me alone? There has to be someone else you could go to . . .

But my thoughts were cut off as Waterman's limousine approached out of the darkness on the street ahead.

It came on slowly. Its lights were off so that it was just a large black shape against the blackness of the trees. It pulled to the curb and stopped. Its headlights came on once, then again. A signal.

I started walking toward it.

I told myself it was going to be all right. I told myself that all I had to do was say the word and I could go back to my life. Okay, so maybe I wasn't a hero. Maybe I wasn't Superman. Whatever. The truth was, I couldn't bear the sadness of leaving my parents, my friends, my girl—maybe forever. I couldn't stand the thought of their tears as they'd watch me taken away to prison for a murder I hadn't done. I couldn't stand the thought of the loneliness that would follow.

As I came near the limousine, the car's back door swung open. The light inside went on, and I caught a glimpse of Waterman sitting in the backseat, waiting. I had an intense feeling of dislike for the man. I wished he'd never come here. Why did he have to come anyway? Why did he have to come to me?

I got in the backseat. I pulled the door shut. The light went out and Waterman became a shadow in the darkness.

I could only make out the shape of him turned toward me. I could only see the dark glitter of his eyes, watching, waiting.

"Well?" I heard him say quietly.

"Okay," I said, my voice catching in my throat. "Okay, I'll do it."

CHAPTER SEVENTEEN

Rude Awakening

Okay, I'll do it.

For a long second after I spoke those words, I didn't know where I was. The limousine, the street, the dojo, the high school—they had all seemed so real that my mind couldn't take in the fact that they had vanished like a dream. But they had. They were suddenly gone completely.

My sense of my own presence seeped into my consciousness slowly. It was not a good feeling. My head was throbbing. My stomach was turning. My body was bruised and aching from its fall off the rock to the forest floor. Leaves and sticks and pebbles were pressing pain-fully into the side of my face.

With a sense of growing misery, I began to remember where I was. My home was gone. My family was gone. My life—Beth—everything . . . I was here, in the forest, alone. Armed guards were searching for me everywhere. And all because I had told Waterman: *Okay*.

I couldn't open my eyes—not right away. Maybe I didn't want to. Maybe I wanted to pretend for another moment that I was still back in Spring Hill. But strangely, as the reality of the situation forced itself into my mind, I realized that things were different now than they were before I lost consciousness. I mean, I guess things were the same—the situation was the same—but *I* was differ-ent—my feelings about the situation had changed—and somehow that changed everything else.

Before this last memory attack, I had been pretty much on the brink of despair. I'd felt sorry for myself. I'd been angry—angry at God, even—so angry I could hardly even pray except to call up to heaven bitterly: *What do I do now?*

But remembering that day—that awful day of deci-sion before I'd made my choice, before I'd told Waterman *okay*—made me feel different.

Because now I knew: I had chosen to do this thing. I had chosen the path that had led me here and I had chosen it, *knowing* that it might lead here. I had loved Beth and I had left her behind. I'd loved my parents and I'd left them behind. I'd loved my friends and my home and my life, even though I hadn't really realized how much I loved them—and I'd left them all behind.

And here was the thing, the weirdest thing: I'd left them behind *because* I loved them. Beth and my parents and my friends and my life—my free, American life. I loved them, and if I had a chance to protect them from the people who wanted to destroy them, then I had to take that chance even if it meant I would never see them again. I hadn't asked for that chance. It wasn't fair that it had fallen to me. It wasn't fair that it had all gone wrong and left me in this place, in this hardship and danger. It wasn't even fair that these people—the Homelanders— had organized to attack us, to hurt us, to kill us . . .

But life doesn't do fair. I don't know why it's that way, but it sure is. I mean, it wasn't fair that I got to grow up in a nice, safe community, while some other kid in some other place was maybe getting shot at or couldn't get enough to eat. It wasn't fair that I had a happy home with parents who loved each other while Alex's mom and dad couldn't stay together. A lot of things aren't fair and I don't think they ever will be, not in this life, I mean.

I understood all that when I got in the limousine with Waterman. I made my choice *because* I understood it. I knew it wasn't about things being fair. It wasn't about them being easy or safe. It was about who I was, who I wanted to be, what I wanted my life to be about, what I wanted to stand for, live for, even die for if I had to. It was about what I wanted to make out of this soul God gave me.

So I wasn't angry anymore. I wasn't bitter anymore. I wasn't in despair. *What am I supposed to do now?* wasn't much of a prayer, I guess. But God had answered it anyway, because that's what he's like. I knew now what I was supposed to do. I knew exactly.

I was supposed to keep fighting. I was supposed to keep going, as long as I could, as far as I could. I was supposed to refuse to give in. I didn't know if I was going to win in the end. I didn't even know if I was going to survive. But I knew that I was supposed to look at this situation I was in right now—look at this trap that seemed to have no way of escape—and I was supposed to find a way—or die trying—for the sake of the people I loved.

With a new determination in me, I opened my eyes.

The Homelander guards—five of them—were standing in a circle around me where I lay on the forest floor. They had their machine guns trained on me. They had their fingers on the triggers.

I stirred slowly. I became aware of footsteps crunching through the nearby brush. The next moment, as I started to sit up, the sixth Homelander, Waylon, came storming out of the forest to join the others.

He walked straight past the guards without stopping. He stood over me as I struggled to rise.

He smiled. Then he let out a single curse and kicked me in the face, sending me spiraling back into unconsciousness.

PART III

CHAPTER EIGHTEEN

Handlebar and Blond Guy

Slowly, I lifted my head. It felt like trying to lift a block of cement. I groaned as a bolt of pain shot through me, right behind my eyes. I could feel the drying, sticky blood stiffening on the side of my face. I tried to move. My hands were caught behind me. Curling my fingers around I could feel the duct tape wrapped around my wrists, holding my arms in place.

I gave a start as it all came back to me. The Homelanders surrounding me. Waylon kicking me . . .

"Take it easy, punk. Unless you want to get hit again."

I turned to my left. It was the blond guard who'd spoken—the one M-2 had blasted in the forest. The burn mark was still there, right in the center of his forehead. I remembered how his eyes had looked angry and mean on the bunker monitor. It was worse up close like this. Up close, his eyes were fiery pools of rage and cruelty.

I was in the backseat of a car, a midsize sedan. We were climbing up a winding, narrow road along what looked like the side of a mountain. There was forest rising at one window: green pine trees interspersed with winter-gray oaks and maples. At the other window, there was nothing but open space as if we were on the edge of a sharp drop.

I was sitting in the middle of the seat. The blond guard was to my left, the guard with the handlebar mustache was to my right. Up in front, the stocky guard—the one M-2 had taken out by the bunker entrance—was driving. Through the windshield, I could see another car on the road up ahead. I guessed the rest of the Homelanders were in there, including Waylon himself.

There was a squawk of static. The driver spoke into his shoulder mike.

"He's awake."

A voice—Waylon's thick guttural accented voice—came

back at once: "If he tries anything, bust him up. And I mean anything."

Suddenly, there was a knife pressed to the side of my face. It was a wicked-looking dagger, the blade thick and sharp. The metal was cold against my bloodied skin, and the sharp edge dug into me. I couldn't move my head without getting cut. I could only shift my eyes toward the guard with the handlebar. He was the one holding the knife.

"You hear that, tough guy? If you try anything, we're gonna start cutting off pieces of you and feeding them to the squirrels out there."

I didn't answer. He pressed the blade against me even harder—so hard I thought it would slice into me.

"You hear me?"

"I hear you," I said.

With that, he pulled the knife away. I watched as he pushed his khaki jacket open and slipped the blade into a holster on his belt.

The car continued to climb. I rocked back and forth as we went quickly around one curve and then switch-backed into another.

"Where are we going?" I said.

"Shut up," said Handlebar.

"I'm just asking," I said. I didn't want him to think I was intimidated by him. I *was* intimidated by him, but I didn't want him to think so.

"We're going to a place where no one can hear you scream," said the blond guard with vicious pleasure. "You're gonna be doing a lot of screaming and we don't want to disturb the neighbors."

"Hey, knock off the conversation," said Handlebar.

"I'm just saying," said the blond guy, smirking. "I'm just giving him a little preview of what happens next."

For a couple of minutes after that, I kept silent. I was thinking—or trying to think. It isn't easy to stay focused when you're scared out of your wits. But I was thinking: the last time I was in the clutches of these jokers, they were torturing me. Now it sounded as if they were planning to torture me again. So the question was: Why? Why take the time to rough me up? Why didn't they just kill me the way they'd killed Waterman? They must be after information. But what was it they thought I knew?

I tried to go into my memory to get at the answer, but the pathways into the past seemed to still be blocked. Despite my memory attacks, my brain seemed to be giving up its information bit by bit at its own pace. There was *something*, though. Something I'd heard more recently, something I hadn't been paying attention to at the time . . .

The car turned hard as we hit another sharp switchback in the road. I didn't have a seat belt on and I was forced over until my shoulder pressed into Handlebar. At the window for a moment, there was nothing visible but blue sky.

Then the car straightened and we continued our racing climb up the mountain. I had to shift in my seat to sit upright. Handlebar gave me an irritated push, helping me along.

I decided to start talking again, see if I could get some hints about what the Homelanders were after. I had to try anything I could to get out of this and with my hands tied, I didn't have a lot of options.

"So what're you guys, sadists or something?" I asked—I tried to put a sneer in my voice as I said it. I thought maybe if I could taunt them a little, I could make them angry enough to answer. "What, do you just torture people for the fun of it?"

"I thought I told you to shut up," said Handlebar darkly.

"Hey, I'm just making conversation. You know, to pass the time during the drive. Otherwise I'll have to start singing '99 Bottles of Beer on the Wall.'"

"You do, and I'll cut your throat."

I smiled. It wasn't easy: I didn't feel much like smiling. Plus my face hurt, and smiling didn't help it any. "You're not gonna cut my throat," I said with more confidence than I felt.

Handlebar pushed back the side of his jacket to show me the knife in its holster again. "Oh no?"

I manufactured another sneer. "No. It's like your friend over there said, you're taking me somewhere to work me over. That means you want to know something. Unless you're just one of those weirdos who likes beating up on people . . ."

Handlebar turned away, refusing to answer, but the blond guy said, "I'll like it. I'll like doing it to you. I owe you for blasting me with that gizmo. So yeah, I'll enjoy making you talk. And you will talk, believe me."

"Wow," I said. "You're a real tough guy when you're surrounded by friends with guns."

Blond Guy's eyes flashed and he drew back his fist as if to hammer me.

But Handlebar shut him down. "That's enough," he said. "Now shut up, both of you." He seemed to have kind of a limited vocabulary.

Blond Guy lowered his fist. I went back to thinking. I

was right, I thought, they did want information. But what?

And now I remembered . . . Something Waylon had said to me just before the bunker had blown up. I had been so keyed up waiting for the explosion that I'd barely noticed it at the time. Then, afterward, focused on my effort to escape, I'd forgotten all about it.

It was something Waylon said when he was taunting me. *There's only one other person who knows about you at all. And before you die—which will be in agony, by the way—you're going to tell me who he is, and you're going to die knowing that I'm going to kill him too.*

It's always amazing to me how just when things seem to be impossibly bad, impossibly dark, some distant light shines through, some little handhold you can grab to keep from going completely under. Here I was, helpless, tied up, being spirited away to some place where these clowns were planning to torture me to death, and suddenly I realized: *Waterman and his crew weren't the only ones, after all. There must be someone else who knows my mission, someone who can help me and clear my name.*

For a moment or two, I racked my brain, trying to think of who it might be, but the name just wasn't there. It wasn't there *yet* anyway. If the drug Waterman gave me kept doing its trick, if I kept having these memory attacks, eventually the whole story would come back to me—maybe even including the name of my ally.

The car continued its winding climb up the mountainside. No other cars passed us. No other cars came up behind. We must've been pretty far from civilization at this point. There didn't seem to be anyone else around.

I wondered how long it would take us to reach our destination, how much time I had before they started to work on me.

I turned to Handlebar. "You know what your problem is?" I said.

His face contorted with anger. "I thought I told you . . ."

"To shut up, yeah, I know."

"Well, do it then."

"You're not much of a conversationalist, are you?"

He only snorted at that.

"All right, never mind. If you don't want to know, I won't tell you. You'll go to your grave never knowing what's wrong with you."

Handlebar laughed. It wasn't a nice laugh. "Man, you are really something, aren't you? You are really asking for it."

I was. I knew I was making these guys angrier and angrier. But if I got them angry enough maybe they'd make a mistake, blurt something out. Sure, maybe they'd kill me too. But what other choice did I have? I wasn't going to just sit there and wait for them to start cutting me up.

"Your problem is you're stupid," I told him.

The way Handlebar bared his teeth, I thought he was going to take a bite out of me.

"Hey, I mean that in the nicest possible way," I told him. "I mean, I'm just trying to be helpful here."

"Is that right?" he said through his bared, gritted teeth.

"Yeah. Really. See, you guys think I'm some sort of traitor to the cause or something, right? You think if you torture me, I'll tell you the names of all the other traitors . . . or something like that anyway."

"And?" said Handlebar—I'd hooked him now. He was actually interested in what I was saying.

"Well, the thing is, maybe I am a traitor. Maybe there are all kinds of people infiltrating your organization every which way. But it doesn't matter."

"Oh no? Why's that?"

"Because I can't remember, you knucklehead. I can't remember anything that happened for the last year."

At that, Handlebar's eyes shifted. Interesting: he was looking across me at Blond Guy, as if they were sharing some sort of information between them.

"You already know that, don't you?" I said. It was a guess, but I could tell by the look on Handlebar's face that I was right. They already knew all about my amnesia. Of course they did. I had told Mr. Sherman about it. And these were probably the guys who had found Sherman where I'd left him in the haunted mansion. These were the guys who had tortured and killed him there. They would have made sure he told them everything he knew before he died.

I could see some of this playing out in Handlebar's eyes and I said, "That's right. Sherman was telling you the truth. I don't remember anything."

Handlebar started at that. He didn't like me reading his mind. He said, "Sherman told us what you told him. That doesn't make it the truth. I mean, if you're not a traitor, what were you doing with Waterman?"

"Good question. I was with Waterman because he shot me up with a drug and carted me off to his underground playroom where—guess what?—he was trying to get information out of me too."

I could see Handlebar working that over in his none-too-bright brain.

"I couldn't help him anymore than I can help you," I said. "Because I don't remember anything. Am I a traitor to your cause? Man, I don't even know what your cause is. Waterman said you were Islamic extremists. Maybe that guy Waylon is, but you guys . . ."

It was Blond Guy who answered me, his voice full of bitterness. "We just want a little fairness in this world, that's all."

"Fairness," I said, trying to draw him out. "Sure. Who doesn't want fairness? I mean, like, it's no good that other people have stuff you don't."

Blond Guy's whole face contorted with anger. "That's right," he said. "It's not. People like Waterman, they're always talking about freedom, about liberty. Big words. But when people are free, they don't do what's right. The way the world works: just because some guy knows somebody or gets born with rich parents or something, he gets all the breaks."

"Right, right," I said. I looked Blond Guy over. With his long, rangy body he looked like some kind of athlete. A basketball player maybe, or a runner. "Like, one guy has connections and makes the team; another guy gets cut."

"That's right," he said heatedly. "That's it exactly. There's no fairness anywhere. People are just totally corrupt."

"But you guys are gonna change all that, huh," I said. "You're going to make people be good."

"That's right," said Blond Guy heavily.

"Sure," I said. "Only the problem is, if you make someone good, he isn't really good, is he? He didn't choose to be good. He's just a slave, doing what you tell him . . ."

Blond Guy was about to answer, but Handlebar reached around with one massive hand and grabbed me by the throat. I think if he hadn't been afraid of Waylon, he'd've choked me to death right then and there. But he only clutched at me for a second, while I gagged helplessly. Then he pushed me away so that I fell against Blond Guy—who pushed me right back.

"Now will you shut up?" said Handlebar.

I swallowed hard, trying to get rid of the pain in my throat. "Sure," I said finally. "Sure. I'm just trying to tell you: You can torture me all day long, it won't get you anywhere. I just don't remember."

"You'll remember," said Blond Guy darkly. "We'll *make* you remember."

Handlebar just turned away again and looked out the window sullenly.

I looked out too. I could see a view of mountains beyond the edge of the road, a rolling sea of blue-green conifers and brown-gray hardwoods stretching out into the distance. I thought again about how lonely it was up here. Far from anywhere, far from anyone. There was no one around who could help me.

And then, all of a sudden—maybe there was.

I think I was the first one to hear it—and I didn't believe my own ears right away. We seemed to be so far from civilization, so far from anything, that what I thought I was hearing didn't make sense, didn't fit in.

But a second later, Handlebar stiffened in the seat next to me.

"You hear that?" he said.

Blond Guy listened. He shook his head. But then he said, "Oh, wait . . ."

Then the driver chimed in, "Hey, you hear that?"

And we all sat silently another second, listening.

There was a siren. Far in the distance. But closing on us, closing fast. Whatever it was, it was traveling at high speed over the winding, climbing road behind us.

Excitement woke up in me. It felt like a bird fluttering to life in my chest. Maybe it was the police. Maybe they knew about us. Maybe they were coming to rescue me. All right, that meant I'd get arrested, but getting arrested sounded a whole lot better than being tortured to death . . .

"Could just be an ambulance or something," said Blond Guy.

There was another crackle of static. The driver spoke into his shoulder mike again. "We hear a siren."

Waylon's voice came back at once. "Yes, I hear it too. You see anything coming up behind you?"

The driver checked his rearview mirror. I saw his worried eyes reflected there. "Nothing," he said into the mike. "The road winds around too much. I don't have much of a view."

A pause. The siren grew louder. It was unmistakable now.

Then static—and Waylon's voice: "We're going to go on ahead. Stay behind until you have a visual, then call."

"Great," muttered the blond guy.

"Shut up," said Handlebar, his all-purpose response.

I looked ahead through the windshield. For a moment I saw the rear fender of the green car ahead of us—Waylon's car. Then the green car started speeding up, pulling away. Another second or two and it was gone around the next bend in the road, out of sight.

Good old Waylon. He was running for it. He was leaving his henchmen behind to deal with whatever was coming up in back of us. Nice guy.

So we were alone in the sedan now. Everything was tension and silence—silence and listening. The siren grew louder and louder behind us. I squirmed around, looking back over my shoulder through the rear window. But the driver was right: the road was so twisty, there wasn't much of it visible.

The driver must have been thinking the same thing. He let out a curse. "It'll be right on top of us before we can see it."

"Just keep driving," Handlebar ordered. "It may be nothing. An ambulance, a fire truck. Even if it's the cops, they may not be after us. How would they even know we were here?"

It was a good question. Would Waterman have called the police? I didn't think so. His organization was so secret even the cops didn't know it existed. The hope fluttering in my chest began to fall off a little. Maybe Handlebar was right. Maybe it was just an ambulance or something, something that had nothing to do with us.

But all the while, the siren grew louder.

The sedan pulled around another bend in the road. I strained to look behind me, but nothing was there.

And then, with startling quickness, there it was: a

police car pulled into view, its sirens wailing, its red and blue lights whirling, flashing.

The sedan exploded with noise. The siren. The cursing of the guards on either side of me. The driver shouting into his microphone, his voice high with panic.

"It's a cop!"

And Waylon's guttural shout coming back over the speaker at once:

"Lose him!"

At that, the driver hit the gas.

straining as it climbed the steep slope. I took the opportunity to twist in my seat again, to look behind me again. There was the cop car—a state highway patrol cruiser—just coming out of the turn ahead, keeping pace with us.

An amplified voice came booming out of the cruiser's speakers: "Pull over! Police!"

That was all the Homelanders needed to hear. Handlebar leaned out the window with his machine gun and let out a rattling blast. The smell of gunpowder drifted back into the car to me.

Behind us, the cruiser swerved as the police realized they were being fired on. It careened wildly toward the side of the road, its tires kicking up dirt as they neared the edge. Another inch or two and the cruiser would go over the side, tumbling off the mountain.

I turned to look through the windshield. Another switchback was coming at us up ahead. That would get us out of firing range of the police anyway.

Then a thought flashed into my mind. I glanced over at Handlebar.

He was still leaning out the window to shoot at the police. His body was turned awkwardly, his side exposed. The holster with the dagger in it was exposed. Out of my reach for now, but I started to think . . .

Maybe, in all the panic and confusion, I could get my hands on it.

And then we hit the turn, fast, and once again my body was flung against Handlebar's. And as we straightened out, he lost his position in the window and toppled back into the car, the two of us scrunched up together.

On a chance, my bound hands strained, my fingers wriggled, trying to find the knife handle. But it was no good. I was all out of position. I had no chance to get hold of it.

The car straightened out. Handlebar shoved me off him roughly. I bumped into Blond Guy, who also pushed me away.

I looked out the windshield. We sped on, trees to the left of us, a fall into nothingness to the right. Another curve coming up in the distance.

I would have to prepare myself better this time if I was going to get hold of that knife.

For the next second or two, the sedan shot forward over the straightaway. My heart was pounding hard, waiting for what I knew would come next.

"There he is," said Handlebar.

Sure enough, the cruiser came speeding around the bend behind us. Once again, Handlebar leaned out his

CHAPTER NINETEEN
Car Chase

Helpless, my hands bound behind me, I was hurled hard to the right as the car sped up into the sharp turn. I slammed against Handlebar's body as he reached down to lift his machine gun from the floor. To my left, Blond Guy was lifting his gun too from where it was wedged in beside the seat. As I straightened, they each pressed the button to lower their windows. My mouth went dry as I realized: they were going to open fire on the police.

The sedan went into a straightaway, its engine

straining as it climbed the steep slope. I took the opportunity to twist in my seat again, to look behind me again. There was the cop car—a state highway patrol cruiser—just coming out of the turn ahead, keeping pace with us.

An amplified voice came booming out of the cruiser's speakers: "Pull over! Police!"

That was all the Homelanders needed to hear. Handlebar leaned out the window with his machine gun and let out a rattling blast. The smell of gunpowder drifted back into the car to me.

Behind us, the cruiser swerved as the police realized they were being fired on. It careened wildly toward the side of the road, its tires kicking up dirt as they neared the edge. Another inch or two and the cruiser would go over the side, tumbling off the mountain.

I turned to look through the windshield. Another switchback was coming at us up ahead. That would get us out of firing range of the police anyway.

Then a thought flashed into my mind. I glanced over at Handlebar.

He was still leaning out the window to shoot at the police. His body was turned awkwardly, his side exposed. The holster with the dagger in it was exposed. Out of my reach for now, but I started to think . . .

Maybe, in all the panic and confusion, I could get my hands on it.

And then we hit the turn, fast, and once again my body was flung against Handlebar's. And as we straightened out, he lost his position in the window and toppled back into the car, the two of us scrunched up together.

On a chance, my bound hands strained, my fingers wriggled, trying to find the knife handle. But it was no good. I was all out of position. I had no chance to get hold of it.

The car straightened out. Handlebar shoved me off him roughly. I bumped into Blond Guy, who also pushed me away.

I looked out the windshield. We sped on, trees to the left of us, a fall into nothingness to the right. Another curve coming up in the distance.

I would have to prepare myself better this time if I was going to get hold of that knife.

For the next second or two, the sedan shot forward over the straightaway. My heart was pounding hard, waiting for what I knew would come next.

"There he is," said Handlebar.

Sure enough, the cruiser came speeding around the bend behind us. Once again, Handlebar leaned out his window, Blond Guy leaned out his. They both brought their machine guns to bear on the cruiser. And they both opened fire.

I didn't look back to see what happened. I just looked down at Handlebar's belt, trying to figure out how I could position myself to be within reach of that knife when the next curve threw us together. It was going to be tough—but with a little thought, a little intention, it wouldn't be impossible.

Through the windshield, I saw the next sharp switchback in the road approaching. I knew it would throw me over toward Handlebar and that he'd tumble back into the car as we came out of the bend, just like before.

I was ready for it.

Then there was an enormous hollow roar. I looked back. One of the troopers was leaning out the window of the cruiser with a shotgun leveled at us. He had taken a shot and I could hear the slugs riddling the sedan's trunk.

Now it was the sedan's turn to swerve—the driver's natural reaction to being shot at. He let out another panicky curse as we skidded to one side. Emptiness pressed up close to the window as we neared the edge of the road. Then we skidded back until we were right up against the forest.

Handlebar and Blond Guy both pulled inside, both dodging out of the way of the shotgun fire.

Then the trooper fired again. The rear window blew out. Handlebar, Blond Guy, and I all ducked down, the glass raining down on us.

And then we hit the next curve.

We were all thrown hard to the side—me into Handlebar—Blond Guy into me—the three of us jumbled together. I twisted my body to get my hands on that knife. I felt my fingertips scrape the handle of it. I caught hold of it.

There was a loud *blam!* and a spattering impact and the windshield cracked and the siren roared and the police lights flared behind us as the police car came back into sight.

Both Handlebar and Blond Guy lunged toward their windows, leaned out, opened fire. I heard the screech of brakes as the police car dropped back. I heard the two Homelander thugs screaming curses as they unleashed another round of gunfire.

But I forced myself to stay focused. Because I had the knife. I had lifted the knife out of Handlebar's holster, and I was now working it around in my fingers until the blade came up and lay against the duct tape binding my wrists.

Up ahead, I saw a straightaway come into view in the windshield. I glimpsed the flashing lights of the police car in the rearview mirror. I saw the trooper leaning out the window with his shotgun. Handlebar and Blond Guy were leaning out *their* windows with their machine guns.

I began to use the knife to saw through the tape. The blade was sharp. Instantly I felt the stiff material giving way, my wrists beginning to loosen, beginning to come free.

Then—another blast from the shotgun. Handlebar screamed. He dropped back into the car. He'd been winged by a shot and was clutching his face, blood pouring out between his fingers. At the same moment, the sedan went into a terrifying skid, turning full around in the middle of the road.

Blond Guy let out one more shriek, unleashed one more round of machine-gun fire. The cruiser's brakes screamed again. Then the two cars—ours and the cruiser—smashed together on the straightaway. Glass shattered. Metal crunched. The two cars spun around each other like dancers and then spun apart.

At the force of the impact, the knife flew out of my grip and I was hurled off the seat, onto the floor. Handlebar, still clutching his bleeding face, smashed full force forehead-first into the seat back in front of him. In the front seat, the driver's air bag exploded in a blinding white flare, smacking him in the face. Only Blond Guy was able to brace himself, able to hold his position in the jolting, spinning crash.

The two smashed cars came to rest. There was a second of confusion, a second of smoke and silence. Then Blond Guy was shrieking with rage, kicking at his door. The door came open and he tumbled out.

Dazed, I started to climb off the floor. At the same time, I was working my hands, trying to get them free. I could feel the cut duct tape tearing, loosening, giving me more room to maneuver.

I managed to get back on the seat. I could see through a fractured side window. I saw two state troopers come tumbling out of the wreck of their cruiser. I could see one taking cover behind an open door, the other behind the trunk.

At the same time, another cruiser was coming out of the turn behind them, joining them on the straightaway. Its tires screamed, its front end swerved as the driver saw the wreck up ahead and hit the brakes.

At the same time, the duct tape tore apart and my hands came free.

At the same time, Blond Guy screamed, "It's not fair!" and opened fire on the troopers.

The troopers dropped behind their car, then popped up again, their pistols drawn and aimed. They fired back.

Handlebar, meanwhile, lay writhing on the seat beside me. I reached out over him. I pushed open his door.

Convulsively, Handlebar grabbed me. I tried to pull free. He held on with a powerful grip. I punched him in the side of the head. He let out a growling snarl of agony and fell back against the seat.

I climbed over him and tumbled out of the car onto the road.

I fell onto the pavement, landing on my back on the hard macadam. There was gunfire all around me. The cough and rattle of Blond Guy's machine gun was answered by the steady bangs of the troopers' pistols. Through the smoke from the wrecked cars, I could see flashes of fire as muzzles erupted. I could see sparks fly as stray bullets ricocheted off the pavement.

And, all the while, above the general chaos of noise, there came the steady stream of Blond Guy's shrieked curses, his curses against fate and the unfairness of life. It was a wild, unholy sound, the sound of a man completely out of control, completely possessed by rage and a fury for death.

I climbed to my feet and ran, bent over, stumbling toward the edge of the road, hoping to reach cover before a bullet caught me. As I ran, I glanced back over my shoulder—just a quick glance but long enough to see what happened next.

Blond Guy was out of his mind with blood-fury. He was screaming and screaming, firing and firing at the police behind their doors, riddling their cruiser with bullet holes. His rage made him fearless. He was standing clear out in the open, totally unprotected. He just kept screaming and shooting, walking toward the wrecked cruiser, step after step.

He had the police pinned down behind their car. But by now the second cruiser had pulled to the side of the road. Two more troopers were coming out of it with their guns drawn. They dropped behind their cruiser's open doors for cover. They took aim through the open windows, bracing their arms on the window frames.

Then—in that moment I looked back while I was running, bent over, across the road—Blond Guy's gun clicked on empty. You'd think he would have thrown the weapon down. You'd think he would have put his hands up and surrendered. But no. Standing there, right out in the open, with the police guns still trained on him, he tore one magazine from the machine gun, tossed it away and, in the same fluid motion, reached into his jacket and pulled out another. He jammed the magazine in place, chambered a bullet, and was ready to open fire again.

The last thing I saw before I reached the edge of the road was the troopers rising up from behind their cars—two from behind the ruined cruiser and two from the second cruiser that had just come up alongside it. All four of them opened fire at the same time.

I saw Blond Guy fly back, letting out a last blast of machine-gun fire at the sky as the police bullets tore into him. Then he was going down, crumpling to the ground like some kind of broken toy.

I couldn't stay to watch anymore. I had come to the edge of the road. Only a few seconds had passed since the crash. Handlebar was still in his seat, still clutching his bleeding face. The driver was still sitting slumped and dazed behind the wheel of the car where the air bag had hit him. For a moment, I was there at the edge, unnoticed. Beneath me was a steep drop, a sharp slope of dirt dotted with bushes and stunted trees. It ended suddenly in a vertical fall off the side of the mountain.

I charged off the road and down the slope. After two steps, I lost my footing and was tumbling, tumbling toward the brink of nothingness.

CHAPTER TWENTY

Cliff-hanger

I rolled and tumbled, tumbled and rolled—for the longest time, it seemed. It seemed at any second I would reach the edge of the slope and go falling over. Roots and stones cut at me. Tree trunks banged me as I went past. But I kept falling faster, out of control.

Acid fear burned in me as I saw myself plunging toward the edge of the cliff and the sheer drop below it. I looked desperately for something to hang on to. I saw a tree—too far away to reach. But the roots came out of the ground in a great hunched tangle. Maybe . . .

I grabbed at the roots. I caught hold of a small cluster of them. My lower half kept falling, my legs tumbling past my torso. I clung to the roots as I felt my foot go over the edge into open air. But I had a firm grip. I dangled a second, holding on. Then I dragged myself back up onto the solid ground at the edge of the cliff.

Panting, bleeding, shocked, dazed, I tried desperately to get a sense of where I was. I looked up and saw the road far above me. I had tumbled down a long way. I heard another broken round of gunfire from up there and then the shooting stopped.

There were rough shouts:

"Get out of the car! Get out of the car with your hands up!"

It was the police. The law had won the day, and the two terrorists who were still alive were under arrest.

As I lay there, wincing, I saw a dark figure loom up on the ridge overhead. It was one of the state troopers. He was scanning the ground below, looking for me. I could see by the way he stiffened suddenly that he spotted me where I was at the edge of the drop-off, clinging to my cluster of roots.

I saw him turn away and I heard him shout to his fellow officers, "I see him! He's down there!"

I knew I had to get out of there, fast.

I looked along the ridge on which I was lying. The slope was so steep, the edge so close, I didn't think I'd be able to move quickly without falling over. I'd have to keep my grip on trees, on roots, on anything I could find in order to move along. The police would come down and get me easily. Either that, or they might just take a shot at me from the road.

No, the only way out was down—and that meant going over the side.

There was no time to be afraid. That didn't stop me from *being* afraid—it just meant I couldn't worry about it much. Holding on to my cluster of roots, I lowered my legs over the edge. My feet searched for purchase in the side of the mountain. There was soft earth and there were rocks—but I couldn't tell if my footholds were firm or if they would crumble away underneath me. All the same, there was nothing else I could do. I let go of my handhold. I clutched at the earth under my fingers. I began to lower myself down.

It was a long climb and a scary one. Not a straight drop—not the whole way—but not much of a slope either. There was brush to hold on to, and rocks to brace my feet on. But the brush would tear free sometimes and I would have to grab hold of something else fast to keep from plummeting down. The rocks likewise would break from the earth under my feet and tumble down the mountainside, leaving me dangling helplessly until I could find somewhere else to stand.

But slowly, I made my way. When I looked down after a while, I could see the slope easing off a little bit. I could see a place where I might let go of my desperate handholds and start scrambling again. But I wasn't there yet—it was still a dangerous fall. And as I climbed down, I began to feel something—something stirring inside me—and I groaned in terror.

It was another memory attack. I could feel it starting. I could feel that horrible writhing dragon of pain coming to life in my stomach.

My eyes filled with discomfort and frustration. *Not now*, I thought, *not now*. I paused in my climb, clinging to the mountain face. I clenched my teeth and tried to force the growing pain down by sheer willpower. To my relief, it actually seemed to work for a moment. I seemed to be able to make the clutching agony subside a little and recede—the dragon pulling its head back under cover. I was pretty sure I couldn't keep the memory attack away forever. But while there was time, I had to keep moving.

Slowly, I continued my climb down the mountainside.

And now, I heard noises on the slope above me. Deep voices calling to each other. Brush and sticks crackling. I looked up and saw dirt and pebbles pouring over the edge. Some of the debris showered my hair.

It was the troopers. They were climbing down the slope. They were coming to get me.

"He was right there a minute ago," said one voice. "I saw him."

"All right. Hold on. Take it easy, go slow. You don't want to lose your footing and go over the edge. It's a long way down."

There were two of them as far as I could tell. The other two troopers must've still been up top with their prisoners and the dead.

I kept climbing down. The earth kept raining down on top of me as the troopers' feet dislodged it from the slope over my head.

Then the sounds of brush and branches cracking— the sounds of the troopers' descent—paused.

"Man," I heard one of the troopers say, breathless, "this is really getting steep. Maybe we oughta wait for some climbing equipment or something."

"The kid didn't wait," said the other, also panting. "He just went over the side."

"Yeah, well . . . the kid's a kid."

The other trooper gave a weary laugh. "I know what you mean."

A handful of pebbles showered onto me as the troopers started carefully down the slope again.

I continued to make my slow way down the cliff. I flinched as another twist of pain flared in my abdomen: the dragon of the memory attack rearing its head. But I managed to force the dragon down again and went on, moving my hand from rock to root to tree branch, working my feet from one crevice in the dirt to another as I descended.

A radio squawked above me. "Bravo-90."

I heard the troopers pause again.

"This is Bravo-90," I heard one of the troopers answer. "Go ahead."

"It's Rose."

Now I paused too. Rose! Detective Rose. Was *he* here? Was he nearby? The idea frightened me.

Holding on to a stunted tree sticking out of the mountainside, I rested my face against the cold dirt. I was exhausted and, no matter how much I fought it, I could still feel that dragon of pain waiting to be born in my abdomen. I strained to listen.

"Go ahead, Detective," said the trooper.

"Have you got him?" said Rose. I recognized his voice now, even through the static of the radio. "Have you got West?"

"We're on the chase. He went over the side of a mountain. It's pretty steep. We may need some grappling equipment."

There was a pause. Then Rose said, "You have your orders. Do what you have to do. Get him."

"Ten-four," said the Trooper. Then, muttering to his companion, he said, "What's he giving me orders for? Guy's not even in his own jurisdiction."

"I know. He's obsessed with this kid, though. It's something personal."

"Yeah, well, not falling off mountains is something personal with me."

There was a bitter laugh in answer.

The idea that Rose was guiding the hunt for me gave me a weak, sour feeling. I knew the trooper was right: he *was* obsessed with me. He had believed me when I told him I was innocent. He felt betrayed—humiliated and fooled—when I turned out to be guilty. Now I understood more fully: Rose had been *right* to think I was innocent. It wasn't I who had tricked him. It was Waterman and his people, Waterman and his people framing me for murder. No wonder Rose felt like a fool. And then my escape . . . He didn't know it was all arranged by Waterman. He was furious about it all, and he would never rest until he had me back in custody.

Fighting down the growing pain inside me, I began climbing again. I looked down and saw that a new slope rolled out under my feet not too many yards below. I was almost there. Even if I fell now, I'd probably only get banged up a little. And at this point, I was so banged, scratched, sore, and aching, that I didn't think a few more bruises would bother me much.

"This isn't working," I heard one of the troopers say above me. He sounded completely out of breath now. "There's no way I'm going over the side carrying all this equipment. Not without a rope at least."

"Yeah, me either," said the other one.

Then, all at once, the first trooper shouted out to me, "Hey, kid! Hey, West! Can you hear me?"

I didn't answer. I kept climbing down toward the slope below.

"Hey, kid!" the trooper shouted. "Why don't you do yourself a favor and give yourself up? We're in the middle of nowhere here. These woods go on for miles. It's cold.

Eventually the sun'll go down. It'll be dark. There'll be bears. Snakes and whatnot. Come on! Starving and freezing to death—it's no fun. Hey, West! Can you hear me?"

I heard him. And I knew he was right too. I couldn't see anything beneath me but more forest, more trees. I didn't know where I was. I didn't know where I was going. I had no plan.

But I did have a sort of vague idea of a way forward.

I reached the bottom. I looked up. I could see one of the troopers. He was peeking carefully over the edge of the drop. I could just see his head where it stuck out over the precipice.

He spotted me and shouted: "West! West!"

I began to scramble down the slope away from him.

"This is crazy, West," he shouted. "We're gonna get you sooner or later!"

I knew he was right . . . but I kept going.

CHAPTER TWENTY-ONE

The Next Attack

The slope eased as I reached the bottom of the mountain. Soon I was making my way through the woods again, pushing through brush and tangled branches, moving slowly under towering pine trees and past the gnarled, eerie shapes of leafless oaks. The sun was shining in between the large clouds that sailed majestically through the blue sky, but the air was dry and crisp and cold. I welcomed the feel of the cold air on my skin. I was hot with effort and covered in sweat and the chill was refreshing on my bloody face.

As I moved, I could feel the pain building inside me again. I knew it was only a matter of time before another memory attack came on. Before it happened, before it left me helpless and unconscious on the forest floor, I had to put as much distance between me and the police as I could.

My idea was this: if it was true, as Waylon had said, that there was someone else who knew me, who knew about Waterman and his plan to frame me for murder and work me inside the Homelanders organization, then maybe I already knew who it was. Maybe, I mean, the information was already deep down there in my brain somewhere and I just hadn't remembered it yet. And with my memory slowly coming back to me one painful attack after another, maybe if I could just survive until the next attack, I'd remember who my ally was and figure out how to find my way to him.

The problem was, the memory attacks left me help-less. While I was busy lying unconscious writhing in agony and going back into the past and so on, the police—and Rose—would be spreading out through the forest looking for me. I needed to find a safe place where I could go through the whole rotten process in relative peace.

So I kept pushing my way through the tangled branches and underbrush, kept heading downhill, hoping to find a road or a house or even just a cave or something, hoping I could hold the attack at bay until I was someplace where I could hide and collapse and let myself go.

But with every step, I could feel myself growing weaker. I was thirsty, hungry. Every part of my body seemed to ache or sting or burn. Luckily, the forest floor was growing more and more level as I descended. I thought I must be getting near the bottom of the hill.

I paused. I leaned against the trunk of a tall pine, breathless. I looked into what seemed an endless tangle of forest. The sun was pouring down through the branches in yellow columns. As I scanned the scene, I saw, some yards ahead, a beam of sun fall through a stand of hemlocks to land glittering on the ground.

I saw that glitter and I thought: *Water!*

I moved toward the light. Sure enough, a stream was there, bubbling quickly over a bed of rocks. I knelt on the stream's banks and drew the water out in my cupped hands and drank and drank until my head cleared. I bathed my sores, washed the blood off my face . . .

And as I did, I heard something.

I wasn't sure of it at first. The trickling sound of the water obscured the other noise. But I held very still and listened very hard and after another moment, yes, I did hear it: an engine. The sound of a car or a truck on a road nearby!

I leapt to my feet. I crossed over the stream. I moved through the trees as quickly as I could. The engine sound grew louder. I was pretty sure it was a truck now. It was getting nearer and nearer to where I was.

Was it the police coming after me? The Homelanders? Or someone else, just an ordinary citizen passing through? In any case, it meant I was close to a road, close to finding a way out of the woods.

The sound of the truck grew louder. Then I saw it. Off in the distance, through the trees. A red pickup zipping along a road just beyond the edge of the forest. Not the police anyway. I didn't think it was the Homelanders either.

The truck moved along the road, getting closer and closer to me.

Despite all my aches and pains, despite my exhaustion, I broke out in a smile. I moved faster and faster toward the truck. Maybe I could stop it. Maybe I could hitch a ride. But even if I couldn't, the fact was: I had made it. I had found my way. I was almost out of the woods . . .

I took another step—and that's when the dragon of pain burst to life inside me.

The next memory attack struck me to the ground.

CHAPTER TWENTY-TWO

The Last Day of My Life

I looked around, startled. Where was I?

Dumb question. It was obvious, wasn't it? I was sitting at the dining room table in my house in Spring Hill. Where else would I be? I mean, for a moment, I guess my mind had drifted and I had had this strange sense that I was somewhere else, in some forest wilderness somewhere where something unpleasant was going on . . .

But no, everything was all right now. Here I was at home, having dinner with my mom and dad and my sister, Amy, like pretty much always.

And I was struck by how . . . well, just how *pleasant* it was here. The smell of food filled the house. So did the sound of our voices and occasional laughter. Looking down at my plate, I saw we were having pork chops and applesauce and mashed potatoes. Sweet! One of my favorite meals.

But something was wrong. What was it?

I lifted a forkful of meat to my mouth, started chewing slowly, trying to figure it out. My heart was heavy. Why? What was the matter?

Then, as if I were waking from a dream, everything snapped into place and I remembered. This was my last night here, my last night at home. My last night with my parents for a long time, maybe forever.

Tomorrow, I was going to be arrested for the murder of Alex Hauser.

I had agreed to Waterman's plan. I had told Waterman *Okay, I'll do it.* And now the machinery of my frame-up and arrest had gone into operation and there was no stopping it.

Everything is already in place.

That's what Waterman had told me as we'd driven around the hills in his limousine.

It's all arranged. We'll use what pull we have to expedite the trial. We'll get rid of a lot of the usual preliminaries and get you convicted as soon as possible. It's all going to happen very quickly, Charlie . . .

The meat became tasteless in my mouth. My throat felt so thick, I didn't think I'd be able to swallow. Why had I agreed to this? What had I done?

No one will know any more than they have to, Waterman had told me. *Only a very small group of individuals will be in possession of all the facts. We'll get you arrested and convicted as quickly as we can and arrange the breakout from prison as soon as possible. But we have to be careful not to let it look too easy, or the Homelanders will get suspicious. Also, we need to give Sherman enough time to feel he's converted you to his point of view. So in the meantime, you'll have to be patient and look after yourself. Basically, from now on, you'll be on your own.*

As I chewed the meat that now tasted like cardboard, Waterman's voice replayed in my head. But at the same time, there was another voice nattering away almost without a break. It was my sister, Amy. She was sitting across the table from me, talking full speed.

Coming out of my own thoughts, I lifted my eyes to her. Amy was a year older than me. For as long as I could remember, she had been—not the worst person in the world or anything like that—just what you might call a source of unrelenting annoyance. Having Amy for a sister was like having this irritating high-pitched noise sounding constantly in your ear . . . while someone hit you over the head with a hammer at the same time. It wasn't the constant talking that bothered me, it was the constant *emotion*. She was always really, really something-or-other—really, really happy; really, really sad; really, really nervous or frightened or excited. Whatever emotion it was, it was always as if she were experiencing it for the first time ever on planet Earth and experiencing it more powerfully than anyone on the planet would ever experience it again.

"So Mandy is all, like, I *have* to go to college in California, I just *have* to, and her mom is all, like, *absolutely not*, I am not sending my *baby* so far away, and Mandy is, like, I'll *die* because she and Sam are, like, Lovers Till Death and she's, like, 'Mom, you don't understand, Sam is, like, going CRA,' and she's like all, 'CRA? What's CRA?' because Mandy's mom is so basically clueless and Mandy is like screaming at this point, 'It's College Rules Apply! College Rules Apply!' because basically Sam figures he can be with anyone he wants now as long as

Mandy's not in the same state and Mandy is so I'm-going-to-throw-myself-out-the-window . . ."

With her being my sister and all, it was hard for me to judge, but I think Amy must have been pretty. She had long, straight brown hair and a sort of round face with blue eyes, all of which looked okay enough to me. But I think she must've been more attractive to the rest of the general male population than I could see, because guys seemed to fall all over themselves to get close to her. Her conversation was always so full of Johns and Judds and Joes and Daves and so on, I couldn't keep up with which one of them she was ready to die over at any given moment. It must have been because of her looks. It's the only explanation I can think of. I mean, it wasn't her personality, I feel sure about that.

Anyway, this was her last year in high school, and right now she was involved in what to her was the unbearable drama and suspense of applying to colleges, and I guess that's what she was rattling on about. She herself had to get in to some art school in Virginia or she was going to die, just die, and I guess her friend Mandy had to go to California or she would likely die as well. Teenage girls die a lot, if my sister is any indication. Fortunately, it doesn't seem to hurt them much.

Chewing that piece of cardboard meat, I looked at her from across the table. Her voice seemed to fade away and become muffled and distant. The remembered voice of Waterman returned, much louder, clearer, more real to me than Amy's.

You're going to be on your own a lot from now on, Charlie. On your own, in danger, afraid. I'd tell you to brace yourself, to get used to it, but I know from personal experience that you never get used to it.

"The suspense is *killing* me," Amy said. "I swear if I get wait-listed, I'm just going to keel over on the spot . . ."

I chewed the tasteless meat, unable to swallow, knowing it wouldn't go down past the lump in my throat. I looked across the table at Amy. More than anything, I wanted to get up, go over to her and put my arms around her. Strange as it was, annoying as she was, I suddenly realized I was going to miss her.

I will tell you this, Waterman had gone on as the limousine traveled through the hills. *We chose you for a reason. Partly, sure, it's just because you're in the right place at the right time. But it was more than that. We chose you because we know you're a warrior. We know when the going gets tough—and it's going to get very tough,*

Charlie—we know you won't surrender. In the end, that may be all we have going for us.

"You're not eating, Charlie. Are you all right? Are you sick? Do you have a fever?" That was my mom: Saint Mom of Perpetual Anxiety.

I forced myself to smile at her reassuringly. It was hard to think about what it was going to be like for her when they led me away in handcuffs.

"I'm fine, Mom," I said. "Everything's gonna be fine."

I glanced at my dad. He gave me a knowing look as if to say, *That's your mom for you.*

So it went on. It was nothing. It was dinner. It was my family. The usual thing. A week ago, I'd been more than ready to leave; I'd been aching to get out of the house, get out of town, move away, go to college and start my life.

But it wasn't supposed to be like this. Charged with murder. Taken to prison. Dropped into the midst of terrorists.

It wasn't supposed to be like this at all.

Now I was lying in my bed in the dark. For a moment, I wasn't sure how I had come to be here so suddenly. I had a strange double sense of myself, as if I were at once here in bed and somewhere else at the same time, somewhere cold and far away where I was lying on the ground, twisting in pain . . .

Then that double sense was gone and I was just here, now. My last night in my own bed, in my own room. I was staring up into the shadows. A car was passing on the street outside. Its headlights traveled up the dark wall, across the ceiling, down the far wall to the window. Then it was gone. I always found that comforting somehow. It was a sign of life outside, a sign that there were people in my town who would be awake while I was sleeping.

I was still thinking about Waterman. I was thinking about how the limousine had brought me back to the reservoir, back to the spot where I'd parked my mom's car. As it slowed to a stop, Waterman had said, *There's more to tell you, but you don't need to hear it now. Someone will be in touch when the time comes.*

Then he'd offered me his hand. I shook it.

Good luck, Charlie, he'd said. *God knows you're going to need it.*

Now it was daylight. The last day of my old life. The beginning of my mission.

My bedroom was gone. I was outdoors. I was on the paved walkway by the Spring River. It was a beautiful place with grass leading down to the riverbanks and stands of birch trees all along the way. It was also our special place—mine and Beth's. Ever since Alex's death, we had come here to be together, to walk and talk and think things through.

There she was now, up ahead, waiting for me under the birch trees.

It was late autumn. The trees were almost bare. The grass was covered with their yellow leaves. Some of the leaves floated on the river, moving along its slow current. Some drifted down past Beth on the cool currents of air.

The feeling inside me as I approached Beth on the walkway was almost impossible to bear. She looked so good standing there. So pretty, so sweet, so happy to see me. At the sight of her, I thought: *I can't do this. I can't do this.*

But at the same time, I knew I could. I would. I had to.

As I got closer, Beth's expression changed. She must've seen the strain in my face.

"Charlie?" she said, concerned. "Are you okay? What's the matter?"

She reached out to me with both her hands. But I

thought if I took hold of her, I would never be able to let her go. Instead, I tried to put a hard look on my face. I was just trying to seem sort of cold and reserved, but it took so much effort I think I ended up looking more angry and nasty than I meant to.

I stood apart from her. I hooked my thumbs in my pockets, trying to look tough. Trying to *be* tough. I'd been rehearsing what I would say through most of a sleepless night. I'd gone over it as I shaved and brushed my teeth. I'd been repeating it in my head as I'd walked over here. I had a whole speech memorized.

But now, now that I was looking into Beth's eyes, I forgot the speech and just blurted out:

"Look, I don't want to hurt your feelings or anything, but we have to stop."

It sounded rough and hurtful even to me. Beth blinked, confused. Her hands sank back to her sides. "Stop what?" she said.

"Stop seeing each other," I stumbled on. "We can't see each other anymore."

This wasn't the way I'd meant it to be at all. I was trying to make this easy on her, but my smooth speech was already in shambles and these confused little utterances would only make things worse, only hurt her more.

"Charlie," she said, with a little uncertain smile. "What're you talking about? Why?"

I cleared my throat. I tried to sound firm and tough. "Well, because . . . We just should. That's the way I want it, all right? It's—I don't know—it's just getting too serious for me. After a while, we'll go to college or whatever and . . . What's the point, you know? Look, I just think it's the right thing to do. I don't feel the same way about you anymore and I—I just want to end it, that's all."

It didn't sound firm and tough at all. Not to me anyway. It sounded like I was pleading with her, like I was begging her to just turn away, just run away so I didn't have to go through this. I was begging her to spare me the pain of hurting her.

But she wouldn't. She gazed at me. She had a strange look on her face. I had this weird, uncomfortable feeling that she was gazing right *into* me, right into my heart, reading the feelings there. Maybe she was doing exactly that, because now she said:

"You're lying to me, Charlie. I never saw you lie before, but I know it when I see it. Why are you lying to me?"

I felt the blood rush to my head. How did she see through me so easily? How had I handled this so badly after all my rehearsing? Obviously, Waterman and his people should never have picked me for this job. I mean, if I couldn't fool my own girlfriend, how was I going to fool a bunch of terrorists?

"I'm not . . . ," I started to say.

But Beth stepped forward, cutting me off in mid-sentence. "Yes, you are. I know it when I see it. You're not doing this because your feelings have changed. You feel just the same . . ."

"No, I don't." Again, I was trying to sound tough, but instead I sounded like a petulant child. Beth had called me out, and I knew it and she knew it. All I could do was deny it, all the while knowing she didn't believe me. I felt ridiculous. I wanted to turn my back and just run.

Beth pressed home her advantage. "Yes, you do, Charlie. Don't lie." I couldn't even meet her eyes. I looked away. "Tell me what's the matter," she insisted.

I forced myself to face her. I forced myself to keep my expression cold and hard. But I wanted so badly to tell her the truth. I wanted her encouragement and her advice and her help. I knew all this was visible in my eyes. I knew Beth must've seen it there. Still, I kept up the pretense. I had to.

"Look," I told her, "it just . . . It isn't right, that's all. You and me. It's a mistake."

"Don't say that." Where my voice was strained and

false, her tone was simple and straightforward. "You know that's not true."

"You're just going to get hurt, Beth." Now I really was pleading with her. All my playacting at being tough and cold was falling apart. "That's all I'm trying to tell you, all right? I just don't want you to get hurt."

Beth wouldn't let me off the hook. "You have to tell me what's wrong," she insisted.

"Look . . ." I tried again. "Look, I can't. I can't tell you. Okay? We have to end it, that's all. Can't we just leave it at that?"

"No," Beth said. "We can't. I mean, haven't you been paying attention? We don't have the right to just end this. We didn't make it and we can't end it."

"I don't even know what that means," I said sourly.

But I did. I knew exactly what she meant. In stories, in movies, people fall in love all the time. They get all passionate and the music rises and they overcome all obstacles to be together and live happily ever after. But I don't believe that happens to everyone. I don't even believe it happens to most people. I think, in fact, it's a rare thing to find your soul mate, to find the real, lasting love of your life—and, young as we were, I knew, down deep, as surely as I knew anything, that Beth and I had found ours.

Beth stepped up to me. She put her hand on my arm. This time I didn't have the willpower to pull away. "Charlie, look at me," she said. Once again, I forced myself to meet her eyes. "Charlie, this thing happening with us—it doesn't happen to everyone. They say it does in the movies, but it doesn't. It's special. You know that, right?"

What could I say? She seemed to be taking the thoughts right out of my brain. "Yeah," I confessed helplessly. "I know it."

"Then you know we can't just throw it away because there's some kind of trouble," Beth said.

I tried one more time to sound tough, to bluff this out. "I'm not trying to throw it away, I'm just . . . Aw, Beth." I was finished. I couldn't keep it up anymore. I couldn't resist her, or my love for her, or the truth of what she was saying. I bowed my head and dug the heels of my palms into my eyes, as if I could hold in my misery. "I don't even know what to do."

"Just tell me what's happening," Beth said quietly.

The struggle inside me was epic at that point. I wanted so badly to tell her everything, but I knew that if I did I would become useless to Waterman and his people, useless in the fight against the Homelanders.

I was answering her before I even figured out what I

wanted to say. "It's the worst thing," I told her. "The worst thing ever." Now all pretense was gone. I reached out for her. I took her by the shoulders. I was desperate to hold her. "They're coming for me, Beth," I said.

She looked up at me, mystified. "Who? Who is?"

"The police. They're going to arrest me." I nearly choked on the words.

"Arrest you? For what?" Then I saw her figure it out: "For Alex? How do you know?"

I wanted to tell her the whole truth, but if I didn't lie to her now, everything was over. I said: "I know. That detective . . . Detective Rose. He called my dad. They . . . they found a knife. A combat knife. It's the murder weapon and . . . Well, they say it has my fingerprints on it and my DNA. And they say there are traces of Alex's blood on my clothes."

In fact, the call had come after I'd left the house that morning, but I'd known it was coming, Waterman had warned me. And I already knew what the call was going to say.

Beth stared up at me. "There has to be some kind of mistake. I mean, how could that happen?"

"I don't know. I . . ." The urge to tell her the whole truth was almost overwhelming. I closed my eyes, fighting it

238

back. And now, it was as if a dam broke inside me and my feelings flooded through. I couldn't tell Beth the whole truth, but there was a piece of the truth I had to tell her. I wouldn't be able to go through with this if I didn't.

"Listen to me, Beth," I said tensely. "All right? Listen because . . . well, because I need you to get this. I didn't kill him. Okay? No matter what happens, no matter what you hear, no matter what it looks like, I didn't kill Alex. You looked at me before and you knew I was lying. Now I need you to look at me and believe I'm telling the truth."

Beth didn't hesitate, not even for a second. "I am," she said softly. "I do."

"Never stop," I told her. My voice broke as the emotion surged through me. "Okay? Never stop believing it. No matter what happens."

"I won't."

Then I couldn't stand it anymore. I couldn't stand the sight of her face lifted to me, the trust in her eyes. I took her into my arms and held her against me as hard as I could. "You were right," I whispered into her ear. "You were right and I was wrong. The stuff I feel for you—I didn't make it and it isn't mine to throw away. And I won't. I can't."

"I can't either. And I won't, Charlie. I promise."

"No matter what happens."

"No matter what."

I wanted to hold on to her forever—but without warning, she was gone. Suddenly, I was standing in front of my school, my arms empty, my heart heavy as lead. There were police cars everywhere, their lights turning, the red and blue flashing in the morning air.

I looked around, trying to get my bearings. There was Detective Rose, coming toward me down the school's front path. There were other uniformed officers—a lot of them, dozens of them, it seemed like—closing in on me from every side.

The time had come. I was going to be arrested.

I kept turning, scanning the scene. I saw Mr. Woodman, the principal, looking down at me from the school steps, his face tight with worry and concern. I saw the faces of the other kids at school—my friends, acquaintances— pressed to the school windows, looking out at me, watching.

And I saw my mother. That was the worst part. I saw my mother crying. My father was there, his arms around her as she pressed her face against him and sobbed. I wished she could know that I had chosen this, that it was my way of fighting for what I knew was right. I knew she would be proud of me if she knew the truth. Now, she was just heartbroken.

My dad called out to me: "It's all right, Charlie! It's going to be all right! Just stay cool. Don't say anything till we get a lawyer for you! It's going to be all right!"

As Rose continued to come toward me over the school's front lawn—as the other policemen continued to close in around me—I kept casting my eyes this way and that over the faces of teachers—teachers I'd known for years—and the faces of kids and parents I'd known all my life.

Then, my eyes lit on one face that stood out from the others.

Mr. Sherman. He was standing off to one side of the main building. His face—his expression—was not like the others'. The other teachers—the other students too— they all looked serious: sad, worried, even grief-stricken. But Sherman just looked . . . *interested.* As the police surrounded me, he kind of cocked his head to one side and bit his lip as if he was giving the whole situation some very serious thought.

The next thing I knew, they had me. Rose grabbed my arm with one hand and my shoulder with the other.

He forced me to turn around and then grabbed my other arm and twisted both my arms behind my back.

"Charlie West," he said, "I'm arresting you for the murder of Alex Hauser."

"I didn't do it," I said.

"You have the right to remain silent," Rose responded in a monotone. "Anything you say can and will be used against you in a court of law."

I turned to see my mother, crying in my father's arms.

"Mom," I shouted to her. "I didn't do it. I swear."

But that only made her cry harder.

I felt the cold steel of handcuffs closing around my wrists.

"You have the right to an attorney," Rose went on in the same dead voice. "If you can't afford an attorney, one will be appointed for you."

He turned me around roughly until I was facing him, my hands now locked behind my back. His flat-featured face pressed close to mine. I could feel his hot breath on me. His eyes were hot too—hot with anger.

"Do you understand your rights?" he asked me.

I could only manage a nod.

He stayed where he was another second, held me

where I was. We were nose to nose. And now, when he spoke again, the monotone was gone. His voice was a vengeful growl from between his gritted teeth.

"You and I have some serious issues," he said.

Then he grabbed me by the collar and started marching me toward the nearest patrol car, muttering low, angry threats at me as we went.

But all I could really hear was the sound of my mother crying.

CHAPTER TWENTY-THREE

Sneeze

I opened my eyes. The images of the past broke apart in my mind and drifted away like the mist breaks up and drifts away when the sun burns through it. Where was I? I remembered: the woods. I understood: I had had another memory attack. The car chase . . . The shootout . . . The police had arrested some of the Homelanders . . . And now they were after me, searching for me in the woods.

I became aware that I was cold, very cold, chilled to the bone. I was weak too. Completely exhausted. The

244

effort of escaping the car . . . the pain that had been rampaging through me during the attack . . . hunger, cold . . . My body felt like a rag that had been wrung out and now lay tossed away, limp and dry.

I blinked up into the branches of trees, past the branches of trees into the sky. Blue darkness. Blue mist. Night was falling. I figured I'd been unconscious for a long time and now . . .

Now I heard voices.

Catching my breath, I sat up quickly. There were people talking. They were nearby.

"Rose really wants this kid bad."

"You think? He hasn't let me forget it for ten minutes at a stretch."

"I guess we better keep searching then. I mean, the kid can't be far, right?"

"Why not? Why can't he be far? He can be plenty far. He can be anywhere."

"Come on. He's got to be around here someplace."

It was the police. They were looking for me. Judging by the sound of them, they were close, very close. I tried not to make any sudden movements. I didn't want to attract their attention. I turned my head slowly, scanning the area, searching for them. It was hard to see anything through the gathering dusk. The trees were fading into silhouettes. The sky was going purple.

The voices continued, not more than a few yards away.

"This forest goes on forever. He could have gone off in any direction."

"Yeah, you're right."

"I don't care what Rose says. We're gonna need dogs, that's what. Dogs and trackers. I mean, I'm not exactly Daniel Boone here."

"Tell me about it."

I saw them. Or that is, I saw the dark shapes of them moving among the dark shapes of the trees. There were two of them. Maybe the same two who'd come down the slope after me, I wasn't sure. They were no more than twenty yards away, moving in a straight line behind a row of trees. I could make out their footsteps now—shoes on macadam. They were on the road. I remembered the road. I'd been heading for the road when the attack struck me down.

"All right, all right," one of the officers said wearily. "Call Rose and tell him it's getting too dark. We're giving up till morning."

"Me? Why do I have to call him?"

"Well, *I'm* not gonna do it. I'll search all night if I have to."

"Great. All right. I'll call him."

The two figures paused. I heard the squawk of a radio.

"Bravo-90."

As he talked into his radio, the dark continued to gather. I thought if I sat where I was, very still, not moving at all, they might not see me, even though they were so close.

The answer came back over the radio: "This is Rose."

I shivered. My body temperature had dropped while I'd been unconscious. The cold had gathered with the dark. The damp of the ground had seeped into my clothes. I was chilled all through.

"Look," the trooper was saying, "unless we get some dogs and trackers out here, we're never going to find him in the dark."

Another shiver went through me—I realized I was feeling muddy-headed, maybe even feverish. I was getting sick.

And suddenly I realized something else: I was going to sneeze!

I clapped my hand over my mouth. I pressed my

finger up hard under my nose. If I let out a loud sneeze now, the police would be sure to hear me, sure to find me.

"He could get miles away overnight," I heard Rose say angrily.

"I don't know what to tell you, Detective. We've got the roads covered and we've been calling for backup for over an hour. We're way off the beaten path out here. It's tough to reach."

"I know, I know." Rose's weary sigh came over the radio clearly. "All right. Pack it in. We'll get some dogs out there in the morning."

The sneeze continued to build in me. I pressed my lips together.

"Well, that's done," said one trooper.

"Yeah, no thanks to you," said the other. "Our man Rose was not a happy camper. Next time, you call him."

"You're a hero to your people."

"Oh, shut up."

Their voices were getting softer. They were moving away. I could see their shadowy shapes fading into the night.

Then I sneezed.

It burst out of me. There was nothing I could do to

stop it. I forced the noise down as low as I could. The sound of it came out weird and muffled.

The two policemen went silent. Had they paused? I couldn't tell. I couldn't see them anymore in the night.

"Did you hear something?" one of them said. He was farther away now, well along the road.

"I don't know," the other trooper answered in a tired voice.

"I heard a noise."

"It's the forest. You know? There's all kinds of noises. Crickets, frogs, werewolves. It's a busy place."

"Werewolves?"

"Whatever. I'm a city boy."

There was another silence. I sensed them listening to the night, listening for another noise.

"Yeah, I guess you're right," one of them said finally. "It is noisy, now you mention it. We can't just wander around here all night following every sound we hear."

They were moving away again. Their voices grew softer and softer. Soon, I couldn't hear them at all.

I let out a huge sigh of relief. Then I shivered again. I really wasn't feeling very well at all.

CHAPTER TWENTY-FOUR

The House

I walked along the night road. My steps were slow and shuffling. My shoulders were slumped. I was feeling worse and worse with every minute. Dizzy with fever, weak with hunger. Bruised and sore and cold and stiff and tired all over. Sometimes I thought I would actually fall asleep while I was walking. Only now and then, when a car came by, did I really come alert and scramble into the surrounding trees, hiding there until the headlights passed and the taillights disappeared around a bend in the winding road.

I don't know how long I went on like that. An hour maybe, maybe even two. I kept thinking I would have to stop, that I was too tired, that I couldn't go on anymore. But I kept going on. I kept thinking about the long night alone in the forest, the police coming back for me in the morning with dogs and trackers. I kept shuffling forward, thinking, *There's got to be something ahead; there's got to be something somewhere.*

And there was.

After a long, long time, I looked up and saw a yellow light through the trees. I stopped in the road and stood there, swaying weakly, gazing at it. Was it a car? No, it wasn't moving. I went on, stumbling and unsteady. There was another bend in the road up ahead. As I came around it, I saw the woods come to an end. I saw fields stretching out on either side of the road, dimly visible under the newly risen moon. The road fell off in a hill here, going down and out of sight. And just at the brink of the hill, off to one side, there was a house.

It was a small house, standing alone off the road at the end of a dirt drive. The house itself was dark, but there was a small lamppost at the start of the driveway, and another light, a porch light, above the front door.

I shuffled toward the drive. I was limping a little now

too, my feet sore from the long walk. At this point, everything was sore from everything.

I reached the drive and started hobbling down it toward the house.

As I got closer, I saw there were two buildings. There was the little house on the edge of the field, and there was a small barn or shed off to the right of it. I headed for the light, for the house. Whatever happened, I had to get some food.

It was just an old farmhouse, two stories and an attic, with a porch out front. It had white aluminum siding and green window shutters and a sloped roof. I had to grab hold of a post to steady myself as I climbed the three steps to the porch. There was a large window here to the right of the front door. I went to it, pressed my face to the pane. The cool of the glass felt good against my fevered forehead. I peered through into the darkness.

The house was very still inside. I was pretty sure it was empty.

I limped to the door. I tried the knob. It was unlocked and turned easily. Well, sure, why wouldn't it be unlocked? It was out here in the middle of nowhere. Who was going to break in?

I pushed the door open and stepped into the darkness.

Without warning, a snarling, roaring dog leapt at me, its teeth bared.

Terrified, I cried out and staggered backward. But the thing was already on me, its paws against my chest. It barked once more, its hot breath on my face. Then it stopped barking. It sniffed me. It stood there with its front paws on me, panting and wagging its tail.

In the glow coming through the doorway from the porch light, I saw the dog was a golden retriever, one of the friendliest breeds of dog on earth. Also one of the worst watchdogs.

I patted him on the head. "Good dog," I said. And I gently lowered him to the floor.

I found the light switch. I flipped it and a ceiling light came on.

I was standing on the edge of a small living room. There was a couch and an armchair turned toward a TV. There was a wooden cross on the wall and a painting of Jesus holding a lantern to light the night. There were a couple of end tables cluttered with framed photographs featuring a man in a Marine uniform, a woman, and a little boy. All the furniture looked worn and threadbare.

The braided rug looked worn and pale. There was a little work nook in one wall. There was a wooden table there with a laptop standing open on it.

The dog kept sniffing my legs, wagging his tail. I checked his collar. His name was Sport. I ruffled his neck fur.

"Hey, Sport," I said as he nuzzled me. "Show me the way to the food."

Sport knew that word, all right. He immediately did as I asked, trotting happily across the room to a doorway on the other side. I went after him, bracing myself on the furniture as I passed to keep myself upright. When I got to the door, I flicked another light switch and saw the kitchen. It was a wonderful sight.

Sport and I had ourselves a fine old meal. Milk and bread and cheese and those turkey slices that come in plastic containers. I ate ravenously—giving occasional scraps to my furry friend, who also ate ravenously, being a dog. I was glad to be sitting down, glad to be eating. I felt stronger every minute. But my head didn't clear any. In fact, it felt as if my fever was getting worse and worse.

As I ate, I looked around the kitchen. It was modest and small like the rest of the house. There were chips in the light blue paint on the wall. The linoleum on the floor looked old and faded. The refrigerator looked old too.

I saw a bulletin board by the phone against one wall. There was another cross pinned up there and some more photographs tacked up around it. A woman and a boy: the same ones who were in the pictures in the living room. A mother and a son, it looked like. The mother was pretty but tired and faded-looking, with deep lines in her face and white-blond hair that had a lot of strands of gray in it. The son was small and sad-eyed and looked worried, even when he smiled. There were no pictures here of the man, the Marine.

I wondered where this family was now. I wondered if they'd be coming home soon.

Probably, I thought. Anyway, I couldn't take the chance. I couldn't just stay here and wait for them to find me. The police would be spreading the word that I was on the loose. Anyone could recognize me. Anyone could turn me in. Somehow, I had to find the strength to keep moving.

I stood up. For a second I had to steady myself, holding on to the back of the small kitchen chair. The food had made me feel stronger, but I was dizzy; my head felt thick. I shivered and shivered again. Even inside, I felt cold—I felt as if the cold from the forest had eaten deep into my bones. I couldn't seem to shake it off.

I forced myself to let go of the chair. I moved around the room unsteadily, shuffling from place to place. Moving in that way, I cleaned up the kitchen. Wiped up the crumbs. Put the milk carton back in the refrigerator. Before I closed up the plastic package of meat, I took some money out of my pocket and put it inside. It probably wasn't a very smart thing to do. It meant they were sure to notice someone had been here, and they might even guess it was me and call the police. But I could see from the way the house looked that the people who lived here didn't have much money. Even if they did, I didn't want to steal from them and leave nothing in return. I put the cash in with the meat and hoped they just wouldn't think about it too much.

Anyway, I hoped by the time the woman and her son came home, I would be long gone.

"Well, Sport," I said to the dog, "it's been great knowing you."

I patted him on the head. He wagged his tail, looking up at me lovingly. I was sorry to leave him. So many people were hunting me, trying to kill or capture me, it had been good to have some friendly company for a while.

I turned off the light in the kitchen as I stepped into the living room. I hobbled to the door. When I got there, I had to lean against the wall for a minute. I was so weak, so tired, so dizzy I didn't know how I was going to keep going. But I had to. I had to.

Maybe some aspirin, I thought. Maybe I could find some aspirin in the bathroom, something to cut through this fever.

I managed to straighten up. I turned back into the house, thinking to find the bathroom. But instead, my eyes lit on the little work nook in the corner. The desk. The laptop. I forgot about the aspirin. I thought: *Beth*.

My friend Josh had set up phone accounts for us—for me and Beth and our friends—so we could call one another on our computers. We could even see each other if there was a webcam available. It was very helpful when the loneliness got really bad.

I was standing there, thinking about my last memory attack, thinking about how Beth had been able to see right into my mind, read my thoughts. How she'd looked up at me with all that trust in her eyes, believing in me even when I told her I was going to be arrested and charged with murder.

Maybe I could tell her the truth now. What difference

did it make? Waterman was dead. My cover was blown. There was nothing to lie about anymore, nothing to protect. I could tell Beth the truth and she could reach my mom and dad and tell them about it too. I remembered my mom crying as the police came to take me away. It made me feel like someone had taken my heart in his fist and squeezed it. It would be nice if she knew the truth about me for sure.

I glanced out the window. There was no sign of anyone, no sign of lights on the driveway or even out on the road. Maybe I had time . . .

I went to the computer and turned it on. I had to sit down on the desk chair as I waited for it to boot up. I could barely keep on my feet now. My head felt like it was burning up with fever. I stared at the laptop, blinking heavily, my mouth hanging open stupidly. Sport sniffed at my leg and panted, looking worried.

After a second or two it occurred to me I better take a look outside again, make sure no one was coming. I didn't want to do it. It seemed like a long way back to the door. Still, I thought it was the smartest thing to do.

I groaned as I forced myself to stand up. I made my way back to the door slowly. While I was there, I turned off the living room light again. I looked out the window while the computer continued booting behind me. There were still no lights outside, no cars coming.

Soon the laptop was fully working, its screen bright in the dark room. I moved back to the desk by its light, gripping the furniture for support while I went. Sport followed along beside me. I plunked down into the desk chair again. Sport sat down next to me and watched.

I brought up the browser and used it to find the phone program. There was no camera in the laptop so Beth wouldn't be able to see me, but I'd still be able to see her. I brought up Beth's number and called it. I sent up a little prayer that she'd be home.

The ring tone sounded so loudly in the quiet house, I looked over my shoulder at the window to make sure there was still no one coming. The tone sounded again.

Then it stopped. I heard Beth's voice, charged, excited.

"Charlie?"

A swirling image appeared on the laptop. A caption said, "Video starting."

"Beth, it's me."

"I can't see you."

"There's no camera in my computer. Is your camera on?"

"Yes, you should see me in a minute. Are you all right?"

"Yeah, I'm okay. How about you?"

"I'm fine. I've been so worried about you. Did you find the man you were looking for?"

"I found him, Beth but . . ."

I was about to tell her what happened when the video came on. There she was, her living image on the screen right in front of me. Seeing her again . . . it's hard to describe what it was like. Even feeling as bad as I did, the sight of her was like a sort of flash of light going off inside me. I reached out for the screen and touched the image, feeling only the monitor's cool, featureless surface against my fingertips.

"Beth," I said softly.

She smiled. I moved my fingers down over the side of her face, trying to imagine I was really touching her.

"Beth," I said. I could barely get the words out. "Beth, I remember."

Her lips parted in surprise. "What . . . ?"

"I remember. I remember everything. I remember us."

"Oh, Charlie," she said, her voice breaking.

"I remember all about us, all of it."

Beth covered her mouth with both her hands. I heard her sob and say: "Thank God, thank God."

"Everything's starting to come back to me now, soon I'll have the whole story but . . ."

Just then, Sport let out a bark. I turned and saw head-lights flash on the front windows.

"Charlie?" said Beth. "What was that noise?"

The headlights outside grew brighter. A car was approaching up the dirt drive.

Beth said, "Is something wrong?"

I turned back to look at her. I would've given any-thing not to have to say good-bye, but I had no choice.

"I have to go," I told her.

"Go," she answered at once. "Don't worry. I'll be here. Just go. Stay safe."

Quickly, I turned off the computer. I had to close the lid to shut out its light. That wasn't the way it was when I found it, but I hoped I'd be gone before anyone noticed the difference.

I stood up—and the minute I did, I knew I was in trouble.

My head swam. My legs felt as if they were made of rubber. I looked back at the window. The headlights glared in at me as the car grew near. I stood there unsteadily, staring at the lights and, as I did, they grew huge and out of focus and then dwindled to a small point in the dark-ness so that I thought I was going to faint.

It was the fever. It was getting worse, much worse. I

wasn't sure I could even walk—but I had to try. I had to get out of here.

There was no chance of running away. I just didn't have the strength. But I thought if I could get out of the house, maybe I could make it to that shed next door. I could hide out in there until I felt better.

The headlights were right outside now, right in front of the porch. No way to escape through the front door. I had to find another exit.

As the car came to a stop outside the house, the headlights shone in on me through the front window. I could make out the room in the glow. I threaded my way between the chairs and end tables and moved toward an archway on the back wall. I passed through it into another room. It was darker in here, but I could just make out a dining table, some chairs, a sideboard. Another door on the far wall. I took a step toward it . . .

Then the room tilted sickeningly. It felt as if it were going to turn completely upside down and dump me off the floor onto the ceiling. My stomach pitched. I grabbed hold of . . . something, I don't know what. The back of a chair, I guess. My feet felt as if they were anvils. I couldn't lift them. I couldn't move . . .

Now I heard the front door opening. Sport was

barking happily to welcome his people home. The light in the living room went on.

I heard a little boy's high, piping voice: "And then Dan said they'd let me play tomorrow, only they couldn't today because the game was too important . . ."

A woman's lower, quieter voice answered wearily, "Well, that's good. Quiet, Sport."

"Hi, Sport!" said the boy.

The dog's barking stopped and was replaced by happy panting.

I had to go, had to get out of here. I took a heavy step toward the door. There had to be a back way.

I took another step—but I hadn't let go of the chair. I didn't have the strength to let go of it. As I moved, the chair tilted over and fell to the floor with a crash. I lost my footing and stumbled to the side until my back thudded into the wall.

Sport let out another bark in the living room.

"What was that, Mommy?"

I heard the woman answer, her voice tense: "I don't know."

"Is someone here?"

"Ssh, Larry. I don't know."

I tried to move to the door, to get out, but I felt if I let go of the wall I would topple over. The shadows whirled around me. My thoughts were muddy and confused. Red and blue lights seemed to flash in the darkness as if police cars were closing in on me. Somewhere in the distance, I thought I heard my mother sobbing.

"Is someone in there?"

That was the woman, calling from the living room. Her voice was soft, tentative, afraid. Sport came into the archway, wagging his tail. He let out another happy bark, this one at me. I stared at him dumbly, my mouth hanging open.

"Is someone in there?" the woman called again from the living room. "I'm calling the police right now!"

Then the dining room light snapped on.

I saw the woman—the woman from the photographs in the kitchen. She was staring at me from the archway. Her expression was both frightened and stern. She had the little boy clutched against her leg. He stared at me too, his eyes wide and worried. Sport stood beside them, barking and wagging his tail.

"Who are you?" she said. "What are you doing in my house? What do you want?" But her eyes softened as she looked at me. She brushed a strand of hair out of her eyes. "My God, look at you. Are you ill?"

I couldn't answer her. I could only gape at her, dazed. I didn't quite know where I was anymore. I couldn't quite figure out what was happening. There was so much confusion. The lights flashing. The dog barking. My mother crying.

"Mom?" I said then. "Mom . . . I'm so sorry."

And I slid down the wall to the floor.

PART IV

CHAPTER TWENTY-FIVE

Fever

This time the past came back to me in fragments and in dreams.

I was in a courtroom—but the courtroom was bizarre. The angles of the walls slanted in and out as the place got larger and smaller. The judge's bench was huge. It towered above me, seeming to soar up toward a ceiling as high as the sky. The judge was an older man with a lot of silver hair. He glared down at me from his great height where I sat at the defense table far, far below. The defense table seemed to sit in a pool of glaring light with the rest of the court in shadows around me. In that glaring light, I felt exposed and vulnerable, put on display like a butterfly pinned to a board.

I was on trial for the murder of my friend Alex Hauser. Alice Boudreaux, the county prosecutor, a squat woman with frosted blond hair, was marching back and forth in front of me. She was talking to the jury, wagging her finger in my direction. The jury box was sunk in deep shadow. All I could see of the jurors were a dozen pairs of eyes, gleaming in the darkness, staring at me where I sat in the glaring light.

"The defense will tell you that Mr. West passed a lie detector test—and that's true," Boudreaux said as she marched back and forth, "but when you consider the other evidence, the overwhelming evidence against him, passing that test only proves what an accomplished liar he truly is. Consider this: By his own admission, he's almost certainly the last person to have seen the victim alive. He and the victim argued violently before the victim went into the park. Traces of the victim's blood were found on the defendant's clothing. The murder weapon had his fingerprints on it and his DNA." She stopped in her pacing and leveled a finger directly at me. "This is proof beyond a reasonable doubt that the only possible verdict is *guilty*."

Her words sent a cold jolt up my spine. I knew, of course, that it was Waterman who had put the traces of Alex's blood on my clothes. It was the Homelanders themselves, as I found out later, who had planted the murder weapon with my DNA. The whole thing was a frame-up from start to finish. And yet as I listened to the prosecutor tick off the evidence against me, I was sickened by the idea that people all around me were believing her.

I turned to look at them—at the other people in that distorted dream courtroom. I saw dozens of people sitting in the weird, shifting shadows behind me. Even in the dark that came and went as the walls moved in and out, I recognized some of them. People from school, teachers, students. People I'd grown up with. Relatives. Some of their faces were illuminated for moments at a time by spotlights that seemed to shine out of nowhere and pick them out of the dark. I saw my friends—Josh and Rick and Miler—leaning forward intently, listening intently to every word the prosecutor said. I saw Beth, casting me quiet looks and gestures of encouragement whenever I turned to her. I saw my father, frowning angrily at the prosecutor as he watched her moving back and forth across the courtroom.

And I saw my mother. She was sitting beside my father and he had his arm around her. She wasn't crying now, but I could see by her pallor and her unnaturally bright eyes that she was devastated; terrified by what was happening to her son. I felt the terrible weight of her grief and fear. And I felt the terrible weight of my own guilt for having chosen the path that made her feel this way.

Then I spotted Mr. Sherman. He was sitting near one shifting wall. He saw me look at him. He smiled at me and nodded, as if some secret communication were passing between us.

The sight of him made me nauseous. I felt the movement of the shifting, shadowy room inside me as if I were standing on a ship in a raging sea. Some lines from the Bible went through my mind, a passage about sailors in a storm:

They mount up to the heaven, they go down again to the depths: their soul is melted because of trouble. They reel to and fro, and stagger like a drunken man, and are at their wits' end. Then they cry unto the LORD in their trouble . . .

I wanted to cry out to the Lord too, but what could I cry? He knew what none of my friends or family knew: that I *wanted* to be found guilty—that I *had* to be found guilty for the plan to work. All I could ask was that he would comfort the people who loved me, that he would comfort my mom especially . . .

I turned away from Sherman to face the front of the room again. There was the prosecutor, her face pressed terrifyingly close, her features all distorted as she shrieked at me:

"Guilty!"

Startled, I snapped out of the fever dream—but not out of the fever. For a moment, I was awake in a haze of heat and sickness. Where was I? What was happening to me? The room I was in was a foggy, shifting blur.

"Mom . . . ," I heard myself groan.

And I heard her answer, "Ssh. It's all right now."

I turned eagerly to the voice, lifting my hand. I felt a cool hand take mine. I searched for my mother's face. And there she was . . . But wait, no, it wasn't my mother. It was another woman. Blond, weary. Did I know her? Yes . . . at least I'd seen her before . . . But I couldn't quite remember who she was. Still, her voice was gentle and comforting.

"Just lie quietly."

She put a washcloth on my forehead. It was cool and damp, and the feel of it against my burning skin was incredibly soothing.

"Guilty . . . ," I said.

"No, no, no," she murmured. "It's going to be all right."

I shook my head at her. It would never be all right. "Guilty . . . guilty . . . ," I tried to explain.

From far away, I heard another voice: "Is the man dying, Mommy?"

"No, sweetheart," she said. "He's just sick and tired, that's all."

I held on to her hand. "I'm so sorry," I said.

"I know. Just rest."

I felt myself sinking again, falling down and down and down into the foggy world of the past . . .

"Look I'm just asking you to think logically here. I just want you to ask yourself some simple, logical questions about the things you've been taught to believe. That's not evil, is it, Charlie? Asking questions is just what a teacher is supposed to do. Isn't it?"

The voice was murmuring low—practically whispering—in my ear. There was nothing else. Just darkness. Just that voice. I knew the voice, but I couldn't place it right away, couldn't figure out whose voice it was.

"I mean, when you get a different set of facts, you have to reconsider the situation. Right? You might think the sky is always blue or the grass is always green, but if you wake up one morning and the grass is red, well, you have to reformulate your opinions around those observations. Different information requires a different worldview."

Slowly, as if lights were coming up on a stage in a theater, the scene became visible around me. I was in a restaurant. It was in my hometown, but it was not a restaurant I knew. It was a sort of cocktail lounge in a mall. It was dark with black walls, low lights, small tables, far apart from each other. There was a bar where men sat slumped over their drinks while a basketball game played soundlessly on the TV on the wall.

This was not the kind of place I would normally go to. It was sleazy. People sitting around drinking in the middle of the afternoon. But that's exactly why we were here. It was the kind of place where no one we knew would see us.

I turned to look at the man who was speaking to me. It was Mr. Sherman, my old history teacher. Again, the sight of him made me feel kind of ill, as if the room were going up and down on a stormy sea. He was close to me now, sitting right next to me in a booth seat at a small table. He was leaning toward me over our lunch plates. I could feel his breath as he spoke.

"Look, no one likes to abandon cherished beliefs," he went on in that insinuating murmur. "I mean, we all find these old superstitions comforting and reassuring—I know that. No one likes to find out that something he was taught as a child by his parents or teachers might be wrong. But you have to be realistic. You have to consider the facts."

I looked at him. I forced myself to nod, as if I were considering his words, as if he were making headway in convincing me. To be honest, I didn't much like pretending in that way, but that was what I was supposed to do. That was the job Waterman had given me. I was supposed to make Sherman think he was changing my mind, convincing me to join the Homelanders.

But all the while, I could see right through him. I mean, I had taken history from him two years in a row. I knew exactly the way he argued. He would begin by making these broad generalizations that had an element of truth to them. He would say: You have to use your reason. Or: When the facts change, you have to change your opinion. Which, of course, are true statements as far as they go. But it's easy to twist even the truth and use it for false purposes.

Now Sherman went on, murmuring in my ear: "As

long as you were living your safe, middle-class life, you thought everything in America was perfect. You were all full of big words like 'liberty and justice for all,' and you thought that was the situation you were in. But now things have changed. Now you're being falsely accused, aren't you? You're being railroaded into prison for a murder you didn't commit. And all of that is being done by the very American system you respected and trusted."

This was such typical Sherman, it almost made me laugh. *You thought everything in America was perfect.* That was just dumb! I wasn't some kind of slaphappy idiot or blind patriot. I knew there were problems and evils here just like there are problems and evils everywhere there are human beings. But over time, no other country has been more free or caused more freedom to spread around the world or protected freedom more around the world. And if people aren't free, what are they? If you don't start with that, what have you got?

That's what I was thinking, but that's not what I said. What I said was, "Yeah . . . yeah, I guess I see what you mean. But what about these people you're with—these Islamo-fascists seem like pretty nasty types to me."

Sherman made a motion with his hand, brushing this objection aside as if it were nothing. "Look, you know me, Charlie. I don't believe in any God or religion. That's just old-fashioned superstitious stuff from another age. But these people are committed to bringing this unfair system down, and that's what I'm committed to also. When the smoke clears, that's when we'll make our real move, that's when we'll turn this country into a place where there's no unfairness at all, where everyone has the same amount of money and property, and where no one says anything hateful, or treats anyone unfairly."

"Because you'll be telling them not to," I couldn't help saying. "You'll be deciding for them what's right and what's wrong and making them do it."

"Oh, hey, Charlie. Don't give me this 'We, the People' stuff, all right? Look around you. Most people are idiots. They can barely put two thoughts together in a row. You want *them* deciding what's right for the country?"

Well, again, I wasn't there to argue with him. I was there to pretend to be convinced by him. So I said, "Okay. So you're saying democracy isn't always such a good thing . . ."

"It's not, Charlie, believe me. It's the wrong way to go. People need to be forced to do what's right."

"But what if they don't agree. You're talking about killing people then, aren't you?"

"No, no, no," said Mr. Sherman—but always keeping his voice low, always keeping his face close to mine so no one else could hear what he was saying. "I'm talking about *saving* people, Charlie. Saving all the people who die because of America's evil."

I would have paid cash money to tell him what I thought of him just then. But I did my job. I said, "Uh-huh."

"Listen, Charlie, here's the thing," Sherman went on softly. "Let's say you get convicted of Alex's murder."

"Well, I hope I won't . . ."

"I know, I know," he said, cutting me off. "But let's just say you get unfairly convicted and sent to prison. You could be forty or fifty before they set you free again. That's your whole life gone, Charlie. For what? For a lie. For nothing. Just because they needed a scapegoat."

I swallowed hard, as if I were considering his words. "Yeah? So?"

"So these Islamic guys you hate so much?"

"I don't hate them. I just disagree with them."

"Whatever. The thing is: they have deep contacts in our prisons, a lot of powerful contacts. If you joined with us, I could arrange for you to break free of any prison they try to put you in. Instead of rotting away behind bars until you're an old man, you could be living free, fighting to make this a better country."

I leaned toward him and was about to answer, but as I did, I felt that nausea again. The way the dark room shifted back and forth and the way Mr. Sherman pressed his face close to me and the way he kept whispering in that soft, intense, insinuating way—it was all sickening.

I shook my head a little, trying to clear it. It seemed to be getting darker around me. It was harder and harder to see the restaurant.

"Okay," I said quietly. "Okay. Just for the sake of argument, if I joined up with you, what would I have to do?"

The light got dimmer and dimmer. The walls of the restaurant disappeared in the encroaching darkness. The darkness spread toward us like a stain, the other tables disappearing first, then our own table getting dimmer. Soon, I could barely make out Sherman himself, even though he was right next to me.

Finally, blackness.

I reached out blindly. A gentle hand took hold of mine. A woman's kindly face hovered over me.

"Ma . . . ?" I moaned softly through my fever.

"It's all right, sweetheart."

"Didn't want to hurt you . . ."

"I know. It's all right."

"So sorry . . ."

"No, you did the right thing."

"Made you cry . . ."

"It's a sad world sometimes. Sometimes people have to cry, that's all."

"Never wanted . . ."

"I know. It's all right."

I clung to her cool hand for comfort. Her face swam in and out of focus. Sometimes I thought it was my mom and sometimes I wasn't sure. I wanted to see my mom so much. I wanted to be home again so much. I was tired of being on the run, tired of being alone.

"Ma . . . ," I whispered.

"Ssh," the woman whispered back. "Just rest."

I sank back into dreams and memory.

⊕

I came into a strange and shadowed place. It was some kind of garden maze, but instead of hedges there were corridors formed by high trellises. The trellises were covered in twisting branches that sprouted thorns, like rosebushes with all their flowers gone. I moved through patches of bright light into patches of deep darkness. Somewhere not far away, I could hear voices murmuring:

"The court is now back in session. Judge William Taggart presiding."

"The bailiff will bring in the jury."

It was my trial. In this dream-memory, it was going on at the same time I was wandering in this strange, barren garden maze.

I turned a corner and stepped into a dark square. I had reached the center of the maze. I thought there was a statue here, the figure of a man. But as I stood and looked at it, the statue let out a sigh. It was no statue at all. It was an actual man, waiting for me in the depths of the maze's shadows. I couldn't see his face. I could only make out his figure.

"Has the jury reached a verdict?" came the voices murmuring in the distance.

"We have, Your Honor. We find the defendant, Charlie West, guilty of murder in the second degree."

There was a loud cry that seemed to go into my heart like a knife.

"Charlie! No!"

It was my mother, her voice rising above the general murmur of the crowd's reaction. Her cry broke off into painful sobbing that went on and on beneath the pound, pound, pound of the judge's gavel.

"This court will come to order!"

The noises of the courtroom faded slowly. My mother's sobbing was the last sound to disappear. Then it was silent here at the center of the dark maze. I stood in that silence with the eerie figure in the shadows.

After another moment, the figure spoke to me: "Hello, Charlie."

I don't know why, but his voice sent a chill through me. I peered at him, trying to make out his face, but I couldn't. Everything felt strange and uncanny to me. I knew I was in a dream, but I knew it was partly real too, partly a memory of something that had really happened to me.

"You understand what's going to happen now, right?" the dark figure said.

I nodded. I shivered. I knew. "I'm going to prison."

"That's right. Not for long, though. The Homelanders have already arranged for your escape. And we've already arranged for you to get away with it."

I nodded. My heart was beating hard.

"Frightened?" the man asked me.

I shrugged. I guess I was frightened a little. And sad too—sad about my mom and all the pain I was putting her through. But there was something else as well. I was excited. I was ready for the mission to begin, ready for the fight to begin, ready to do what I had been called to do.

"I'll be all right," I told the shadowy man.

The man's voice grew grim. "You're going into a dangerous world, Charlie. A world full of twisted people with twisted philosophies. They will try to use you to commit any atrocity they can. And if, for even a second, they suspect you're not completely on their side, they will kill you without a second thought."

I put my hands in my pockets, lifting my shoulders around my ears. "I know all that. I'm ready."

I could feel the man smile in the darkness. "I'm sure you are. You're a special guy, Charlie. That's why we came to you in the first place." He stepped toward me. Again, I strained against the shadows, trying to see him. I could just make out the outline of his features. "And now, before they take you away, there's one last thing I have to tell you. A technician is going to come to you in your cell.

He's going to install a device inside your mouth. The device can be activated by a sound code, which he'll teach you. When the device is activated, it will release a chemical for you to swallow . . ."

I stared at him. "What do you mean? Like a suicide pill? In case I get captured and tortured or something?"

"It *is* in case you get captured and tortured. And it *is* a pill of sorts. But it won't kill you. We knew you wouldn't use something like that."

"That's right. I don't do suicide."

"Fair enough. But what this pill *will* do is wipe out your memory. That way, no matter what happens, you won't be able to reveal anything about us, the people who sent you, the organization we represent."

I shook my head, trying to understand. "If I activate this device and swallow this stuff, I'll lose my memory? I won't know who I am?"

"No, no, it shouldn't affect your long-term memory. You'll still know who you are. You'll remember most of your life. We're not sure, in fact, just how much of your memory will be erased. The drug is still experimental. But we figure about a year or two of your past will disappear. The point is: you won't remember being sent on this mission or who sent you."

I just stood there in the shadows, thinking about it. A year or two of my life, gone. All the stuff that had happened to me. Beth . . . "Will the memories be erased forever?" I asked.

He gave a small, sad laugh. "To be honest, Charlie, if you find yourself in a situation where you need to use this thing, it's not likely you'll live much longer, so I wouldn't worry about it."

"Yeah, I see what you mean."

"But, just as a point of information? If you *do* get caught and you *do* get tortured and you *do* swallow this chemical and then, somehow, against all odds, you manage to survive and find your way back to us . . . Well, in that very unlikely series of events, we have an experimental antidote to this drug as well. I would say there's a good chance, under those unlikely circumstances, that you'll be able to restore most of the memory that was lost."

I thought about it some more. Then I nodded.

"Okay," I said. "Let's roll."

Then there was one of those sudden shifts in scenery that you get in dreams. I was no longer in the thorny maze. I was back in the courtroom. The bailiffs had my hands pinned behind my back. They were just closing the cuffs around my wrists. I was calling out to my crying mother.

"It's gonna be all right, Mom. Don't be afraid. Everything is going to be all right, I swear. Never be afraid."

The judge's gavel was pound-pound-pounding on the bench.

"The court will come to order!" he said loudly.

I cast a last look back at the people in the gallery—at my mom, at my dad with his arms around her, his face grief-stricken; at Beth, trying so hard to keep from crying as she showed me an encouraging smile; at my friends, Josh and Rick and Miler, tapping their chests with their fists to let me know they were still with me in their hearts—everything seemed to fall away beneath that steady pound, pound, pound of the judge's gavel . . .

Which now became another pounding, a different sort of pounding, somewhere nearby.

My eyes snapped open. I was awake. My gaze roamed over the white ceiling above me. Something was different. I was more clearheaded. I was covered in cold sweat.

My fever had broken.

I licked my dry lips. I turned my head on the pillow

to look around. I was in a small bedroom. I was lying on a single bed against one wall. A woman—the same woman who had caught me after I'd broken into her house—was seated on a wooden chair by my bedside. She was wearing a sweatshirt and jeans now. She looked tired. She smiled at me. I tried to smile back.

The pounding . . .

Even though I was awake, the pounding from my dream continued. I realized now: It was not the judge's gavel. It was someone knocking on the door in a nearby room.

The woman gave a sigh and pushed out of her chair to her feet. Instinctively, I reached for her.

"Ma'am . . . ," I said weakly.

"It's all right," she said softly. "I'm just going to go see who's at the door."

I let my hand fall back onto the thin blanket on top of me. I lay where I was and watched her move out of the room.

The pounding continued. I heard the woman call out, "All right, all right, I'm coming."

I heard Sport add his opinion with a short, sharp bark.

In the next several seconds as she crossed to her

front door, my eyes traveled around the little room. It was bare, stark. Just the bed, the chair, a dresser with some framed photographs on it. No window. No pictures on the wall, just peeling old-fashioned wallpaper with purple flowers. There was a bowl of water on a small table by the woman's chair. There was a washcloth in the bowl—the cloth she'd been using to keep me cool. There was a bottle of aspirin and a couple of empty juice cartons on the floor too. I guess she'd been giving me aspirin and juice to keep me going.

About a million questions were flashing through my mind. How long had I been here? Hours? Days? How long had I been feverish and hallucinating, lying helpless while this woman I'd never met sat beside me and cared for me? Had I said anything to her? Had I spoken in my sleep? Had I given myself away . . . ?

The pounding stopped. I heard the door open. I heard the woman's voice again, "Down, Sport," she said. Then she said, "Yes?"

"Hello, ma'am," a man answered her. With a jolt of fear, I recognized the voice just a second before he said, "My name is Detective Rose. I'm with the police."

CHAPTER TWENTY-SIX

Rose

The words went through me like an electric shock. Rose! Here! Had the woman asked him to come? Had I revealed something in my fevered sleep that had caused her to call the police? Or maybe she just called them because I'd broken into her house. Or maybe she'd just seen my picture on the news and recognized me. All these possibilities crowded into my mind when I heard his voice.

But wait. Now I heard her answer him: "Yes, Detective? How can I help you?" So maybe she hadn't called him at all. I shook my head, trying to clear it, trying to figure things out.

"I'm sorry to bother you, ma'am. A fugitive escaped from the police near here yesterday. We've been searching the woods for him, but our dogs seem to feel he took to the road and possibly came this way."

"A fugitive?" the woman said. "Oh, my."

"Yes, ma'am. I don't mean to frighten you, but he's a convicted murderer. Considered very dangerous."

"Well, I'm glad you don't mean to frighten me, but you're doing a very good job of it anyway."

I started to sit up in bed, but weakness overcame me and I fell back. I wasn't sure what I was planning anyway. I mean, I wanted to escape, but where could I go? I was wearing nothing but my boxer shorts and T-shirt. Even if I could endure the mountain cold in my underwear, there was no window to climb out of. If I tried to leave the room through the door, Rose would spot me in a second. Still, I couldn't just lie there and wait for the inevitable . . .

The conversation at the door went on. I gathered my strength and struggled to sit up again.

"I'm sorry, ma'am," said Rose. "Would you mind taking a look at this picture?"

"Sure. Is that him? Is that the fugitive?"

"Yes, it is. His name is Charlie West."

I waited for the woman to let out a shout of fear and recognition. I waited for her to say, "I know him! He's right in the next room, Detective!"

But all she said was, "Looks like a nice enough boy." Her voice was steady and calm.

"Yes, he does, ma'am," Rose answered. "Believe me, I know. He fooled me once too."

"You say he murdered someone?"

"His best friend. Stabbed him in the chest."

"Pretty cold."

"Yes, ma'am, it was."

As they talked, I managed to push my upper body off the mattress in slow, painful stages. I slid my feet over the edge to the floor. Now I was sitting up, trying to gather enough strength and willpower to get to my feet. I had no plan, but I figured: At least when Rose came for me, I could do my best to get away from him. I could put up some kind of fight, run as far as I could. I didn't think I would get very far, weak as I was, but it was better to try than to do nothing.

"So . . . ma'am?" Rose said, waiting for the woman's response to the photograph.

"Hmm?"

"The boy. West. Have you seen him? Have you seen anyone who looked like him passing by the area?"

I froze where I was, sitting there, listening.

After a small pause, the woman answered, "No. No, sorry. I haven't seen anyone who looks like that. Don't recognize him at all."

"You're sure?"

The woman gave a little laugh. "We're pretty isolated here. If I saw a stranger, I'm sure I'd have noticed and remembered. You're welcome to come inside and look around if you think he might be hiding under the bed or something."

Desperate to get up, I held on to the bed frame and tried to stand.

But Rose answered her, "No, no, that won't be necessary. Here, let me give you my card. If you see anything, call that number, would you?"

"Sure. Be happy to."

"Meanwhile, if you wouldn't mind, I'd like to take a look in your shed out there. Just to make sure he's not hiding on the property without your knowing it."

"Well, you go right ahead, Detective. Look anywhere you like."

"Thank you, ma'am. I'm sorry to bother you."

"No problem, Detective. You have a nice day now."

I heard the door shut. I continued to push off the bed frame until I reached my feet. But the minute I did, my legs gave out beneath me. I wilted to the floor.

A moment later, the woman was back with me. When she saw me lying on the floor, she let out a little noise of surprise and concern. She rushed to my side. Knelt down beside me. She caught me under the arms.

"Why . . . ?" I said.

"Ssh," she whispered urgently. "He's right outside. Keep your voice down or he'll hear you." She tried to get me back onto the bed. "Come on. I can't lift you by myself. You have to help."

I reached out blindly until I found the edge of the bed and grabbed hold of it. With me using all my effort and the woman pushing at me, I finally managed to climb back up onto the mattress. Exhausted, I tumbled onto the bed and lay there, shivering, weak and cold. The woman pulled the cover over me. She sat on the edge of the bed beside me. She laid a hand on my shoulder to keep me still.

"Why did you . . . ?" I muttered again.

She lifted her finger to her lips. I fell silent.

We waited there together. We listened to the noises outside.

I could hear Rose moving out there, moving around the side of the house. I could hear his footsteps. I could hear him pulling open the shed door nearby. For a moment, I could even hear him banging around in the shed, searching for me.

A moment later, I heard the shed's big door close again.

Then I heard Rose say: "What do you think?"

Another man answered him, "Well, the dogs think he went in this direction for sure. But the trail's old and the road—you know, there's been a lot of truck traffic, chemical stuff. It makes it confusing for them. They got pretty tentative about a half mile back. I don't know . . ."

"The lady of the house says she hasn't seen him."

"You believe her?"

There was a pause as if Rose was considering the question. Then he said, "Why would she lie? Why would she hide him?"

"Maybe he's in there, you know . . . with a gun or something. Maybe she was speaking under duress."

"Yeah, I thought of that . . . ," said Rose.

"You think we ought to go in? Search the house?"

There was another pause. Rose said, "It's gonna be dark soon. We're running out of time. West is smart. He knows we'll knock on doors. I think he's a lot more likely to stick to the woods, maybe head north, try to make Canada. Let's go back a ways and search the forest a little more while there's still some daylight left."

"You got it."

I heard their footsteps on the dirt drive. I heard their car doors open and *thunk* shut. Another second or two and the car's engine started. Then they were driving away, the tires crunching on the rocky ground.

CHAPTER TWENTY-SEVEN

Margaret and Larry

I heard the woman breathe a sigh of relief above me. I guess I breathed a sigh myself. She patted my shoulder.

"You'll be safe for a little while, at least," she said.

She rose from the bed and sat down on the chair again, brushing her hair wearily out of her face.

"Why did you help me?" I asked her. "Why did you tell Rose I wasn't here?"

She smiled, but she didn't answer. She just said, "You hungry at all? You must be."

The minute she asked the question, I realized: Yeah!

I was hungry! I was very hungry. "I am, as a matter of fact."

"That's good. That's a good sign. I'll make you something to eat."

"I don't want to trouble you . . ."

She gave a sort of gentle laugh. "It's a bit late for that, sweetheart. You've been plenty of trouble already."

I laughed a little too. "Why did you?" I said. "Why did you lie to Rose? Why did you protect me?"

She still didn't answer. She handed me a juice box. "Here, drink this, get your strength up. You're going to need it."

"But . . ."

She stood up. "Let me go make you something to eat. Then we'll talk. My name is Margaret, by the way."

"Charlie," I said. "Charlie West."

She gave another smile, a wry smile this time. "So I've heard."

She went out of the room. I worked myself into a sitting position. I put the pillow up against the wall and propped my back against it. I stuck a straw in the juice box and sipped it. I could feel myself getting better, stronger, with every minute.

I could hear the woman—Margaret—moving around

in the kitchen, pots and pans banging against each other. It was a comforting sound. It reminded me of being back at home, lying in bed in the morning, listening to my mom making breakfast before she called me to go to school.

I sipped the juice. I listened to the sounds. My mind drifted. After a while, I just sat there in the bed, the juice box forgotten in my hand. I gazed off into space.

I was thinking about my dream. The dark garden maze. The dark figure standing at its center. I felt a stirring of excitement and revelation as the images came back to me. My free hand lifted slowly to my face, to my jaw. I felt through my skin to the place just behind my last molar. Yes. Yes, I remembered now. What the man said in the dream—it was all true, all real.

After the jury found me guilty of Alex's murder, I had been put in a cell in the county jail. While I was there, someone had come to me . . . No, wait. It wasn't just any someone. It was Milton. Yes. It was Milton One—the technician from the bunker, the Asian guy who had had the controller that worked Milton Two. He had come to me in my cell, wearing a white coat. He was pretending to be a dentist. He had installed the device in my gums— the device the man in the maze had talked about. He had installed it just where I was touching now, just behind my teeth. It was a tiny computer. There was a pattern of taps I could make on it with my teeth—complicated and precise so I would never set the device off by accident. But once I did set the device off, it would release an experimental chemical into my mouth. When I swallowed it, the chemical would eliminate part of my memory.

So now I knew. I knew what had happened to me. I had been recruited by Waterman to infiltrate the Homelanders. Because of my closeness to Sherman, because of Sherman's conviction that I could be convinced to join him, because of my karate skills, because of my sure and certain commitment to American liberty, I had been a perfect candidate for the job. The rest I didn't remember yet, but I could guess. I must've succeeded in my task. I infiltrated the Homelanders as planned. But somehow, it had gone wrong. I had been caught. Captured. I had been strapped to the metal chair in that white room and tortured. And in order to protect Waterman and his friends, I had set off the device in my mouth and swallowed the chemical that made me forget a year of my life.

It all made sense now. It all made sense at last.

I thought of myself in the dream again, standing at the center of the garden maze, talking to that murky figure. Who was he, I wondered? Was he Waterman? Or was he the other man, my other contact, the one Waylon was searching for, the man who could still identify me as an agent working for America?

I struggled to delve past the dream images, into my memory. But before I could give it much consideration, I was distracted by something: the smell of bacon and eggs coming out of Margaret's kitchen. The house was small and the smells reached me full force and I suddenly realized, full force, just how incredibly hungry I was. I licked my lips as my mouth watered.

It was only then, as the smells brought me back to myself, that I realized someone was watching me.

Startled, I turned to the door. It was the boy—the boy from the photographs, the little boy who had come in with Margaret when they caught me inside their house— Margaret's son. I had heard his name just before I collapsed. What was it?

"Larry," I said aloud.

He was just outside the door, hiding behind the frame, fearfully peeking in around the edge of it. He was a little guy, his face thin and pale. He had dark circles under his eyes and a frowny, worried expression. When I spoke his name, he ducked back behind the door and out of sight. But after a moment, he peeked out at me again.

"Hey, Larry, how's it going?" I said.

"Fine," he murmured shyly.

I noticed he was clutching something in his fist.

"What've you got there?" I asked him. "You bring something to show me?"

He had. He opened his hand and held it out so I could see.

"Soldiers," I said.

"Marines," he corrected me.

"Marines, right. They're the best, aren't they?"

He nodded.

I remembered the photographs I'd seen in the living room. "Your dad's a Marine, isn't he?"

The boy nodded. "Only he got killed in Afghanistan."

"Wow," I said. "That's really sad. I'm sorry."

"He's in heaven now."

"I hear Marines get to go to the head of the line up there."

That made Larry smile. With a little more confidence, he said, "Because he was fighting for people to be free." And then he added: "Like you are."

Before I could react, Margaret's voice came from the

living room. "Hey there, you. Didn't I tell you to stay in your room?"

Now she came back into view. She was carrying a tray with my food on it. Larry gave the tray the eye.

"I'm hungry too," he said.

"Well, we're gonna eat just as soon as I feed our guest, all right?"

"How come he gets to have breakfast when it's dinnertime?"

"Because he's been sick."

"I feel sick too," said Larry.

"No, you don't. Now get back in your room before I hang you by your toes and tickle your nose to make you sneeze upside down."

"Yuck," he said. "That's disgusting." He gave me a glance.

"See you, Larry," I said.

He waved and shuffled away from the door.

She came in and handed me the tray to set down on my lap. Eggs, toast, hash brown potatoes. I was so hungry, I could barely get out a "Thank you" and say a silent grace before I tore into it. Margaret sat in the chair and watched me shovel the food into my mouth with a small smile on her lips.

"You say grace?" she asked me.

"Yes, ma'am."

"All right. Well, it's good to see you eat, that's for sure."

I answered with my mouth full. I could barely stop eating long enough to get the words out. "How long have I been here?"

"A night and a day. It's getting toward evening again now." She had a soft, kind voice. It was like her face: tired but somehow peaceful. She looked and sounded like a woman who was on a long, hard journey but knew she was headed for a good place.

"You have a nice son," I said to her.

"Yes, I do. Thank you."

"Why did he say that? About me fighting for freedom." She only smiled.

"I guess I've been talking in my fever, huh?" I said.

She nodded slowly. "You have."

I guess I should've been upset about that—you know, upset that I'd given myself away and all. But for some reason, it didn't bother me. I knew instinctively that I could trust this woman. It wasn't just that she'd protected me from Rose or taken care of me in my delirium or that her husband had been a Marine. It was partly all those things, I guess, but it was also just something about her, something about the way she was.

"Did I tell you everything?" I asked her.

"I guess. It was all pretty confused, but I guess you told me enough. It's quite a story."

"I'm only remembering it now myself."

"So I gathered. They gave you something?"

"Some kind of chemical, yeah. It made me forget the last year."

There was nothing left on my plate by this time but the yellow yolk of the eggs and a piece of toast. I mopped up the yolk with the toast and took a bite.

"I'm sorry about your husband," I said.

"Swallow first. I can't understand you."

I worked the toast down. "I'm sorry about your husband."

She didn't answer right away. She nodded. After a moment, she leaned forward in her chair, putting her elbows on her knees and looking down at the floor. "It broke my heart," she said. "He was the best man I ever knew or ever expect to know, and I miss him every day and our boy misses him." She lifted her head and looked at me with a peculiar, intense look. "But now I'm going to tell you something about that. All right?"

"Yeah . . . sure," I said.

"No, I mean, really. Look at me, Charlie."

I looked at her, the last piece of bread lifted halfway to my lips.

She said: "A broken heart is not the worst thing in the world. And neither, when it comes to that, is death. You can't get through a good, strong life without coming upon both of them one way or another, without looking them both straight in the eye. But if I could go back in time and protect myself from my broken heart by living my life in fear, by saying yes to every bully and slave driver who came along, by scuttling away from my duty and from my country and from the things I love and believe in, I wouldn't do it, and my husband wouldn't have done it, and he wouldn't want me to do it. You understand what I'm telling you, Charlie?"

Still holding the toast, I half shook my head. I wasn't sure I did understand.

"What I'm telling you is that your mama is going to be all right. You did what you had to do. And a woman who raised a boy like you is going to understand that one day and it'll serve to heal her heart, trust me."

Suddenly, tears sprang to my eyes. It happened so fast, it took me by surprise, and I couldn't help it, I couldn't stop it. Embarrassed, I set the toast down and wiped the tears away with my palm as quickly as I could.

I was afraid if I didn't, Margaret would come over to the bed and try to comfort me, and then I knew I would break down for real.

She was a smart woman, though. Instead of coming to my side, she stayed right where she was, in her chair. She studied the floor until I was done.

"I hated to hurt her," I said. It was hard to speak. "Until now, I'd forgotten about that part of it, you know. Now that I remember, I remember how much I hated to hurt her . . ." I wanted to say more—a lot more, but that was all I could get out just then.

"I know you did," said Margaret. "And she'll know too one day. But for now, it's better she have a broken heart than a son who can't stand up for what's right when the time comes."

I nodded. I opened my mouth. I was about to talk again when I felt a terrible pain—as if a fist had grabbed me on the inside and twisted my stomach. I gritted my teeth and doubled over.

"Oh, no!"

Margaret was out of her chair and at the bed in a moment. She took the tray away and set it aside. She sat down next to me.

"What's the matter?" she said.

I clutched at my stomach. For a minute I couldn't answer. "I have these attacks . . . memory attacks, I call them. They gave me the antidote for the amnesia medicine. It's bringing back my memory, but it makes me . . ." I grunted with pain. "It makes me sick."

She put her hand on my forehead. Her palm felt cool against my hot skin. "Can you fight it? Keep it off. I don't think your body can take much more punishment right now."

I closed my eyes, trying to will the pain down. As I did, scenes flashed through my mind. I couldn't tell if they were memories or dreams or even memories of dreams. I seemed to be traveling through that dark maze again. It was like a scene from a first-person-shooter video game. The trellis walls with their thorny vines came at me and went past.

Then I was back in the little room again. I opened my eyes.

"You okay?" said Margaret.

I nodded. The pain in my stomach was beginning to subside. "I think it's going away," I said. "For now."

"All right," Margaret said. "I want you to lie down again. I want you to get some rest."

"I think I'm all right."

"I don't care what you think. Lie down," she said quietly. "Go on now. Do as I say."

I let her gently push me down onto the bed again. I watched her face as she pulled the covers up around me. My eyes were already sinking shut . . .

I woke up suddenly. I didn't know how long I'd been asleep. All I knew was I had the powerful sense that something very important had just happened.

I lay in the bed, very still, listening. I could hear the television playing in the next room. There was the sort of silly music and funny voices that usually go along with cartoons. I could hear Larry speaking to his mother—not his words, but the tone of his voice. I could hear the low, warm tones of his mother answering. I breathed a sigh of relief. There was nothing wrong in the house.

What was it, then? Something had happened while I was asleep. I felt a twinge in my stomach and it started to come back to me: more dreams . . . or more memories . . .

Yes. I remembered. I had been back in the garden. Back in the maze. The maze of my memory. I had been in that central square. I had seen the figure there again in the darkness. Suddenly, a light had flashed on. Suddenly, I was not in the maze, not at all. I was in a small white room somewhere, cluttered with shelves and files, brightly lit—so bright that, after the shadows of the garden, I was nearly blind. I was squinting so hard I couldn't even see the man standing right there in front of me.

Protecting my eyes from the bright light, I turned away. There, behind me, were the twisting corridors of the maze again. While I stood there, watching them, a wild thing happened. The maze began to bloom. The stark, thorny branches that covered the maze's trellises suddenly burst into flower everywhere. Rich, bloodred flowers blossoming all up and down the maze's corridors while I stood and stared and then . . .

Then, all at once, I came awake fully. I understood. I had to get to Margaret. I had to tell her.

I sat up. I felt cool, good. My fever was gone. The food and the rest had made me much stronger. I stood—and for a moment, I was nearly knocked over by dizziness. But I grabbed hold of the back of the chair and kept myself on my feet. I waited there until the dizziness passed. After a moment I was fine—strong enough to keep moving.

I went to the door. I rested against the frame. There was a hall, with the kitchen door on the left wall and the living room on the right. It was a short hall, but just then, it seemed to me like a long way to travel.

"Margaret," I called. But my voice was weak, and the sound of the television must've drowned it out. She didn't answer.

I began to move down the hall, bracing myself against one wall, then staggering to the other side and bracing myself there. Images from my dream—or my memory— or whatever it was—flashed on the screen of my mind again. The maze. The white room. The bloodred flowers blooming on the trellises.

I reached the living room doorway. I leaned against it. Margaret was sitting on the sofa with her arm around her son. They had their backs to me. They were watching a DVD. A cartoon movie about fish. Sport lay curled up on the rug, right beside the sofa.

I blinked hard. I looked around me. I could see that night had fallen. There was only darkness at the windows. In that darkness, or over it, like a transparent image, I could still see the trellises blooming in the maze, the thorny bushes bursting with bloodred roses.

"Margaret," I said.

She heard me this time. So did Larry. Startled, they both looked over their shoulders. Sport lifted his head to look at me.

Margaret jumped to her feet and came to me where I stood.

"You shouldn't be out of bed," she said.

"I remember."

"Quiet now. You have to lie down."

"I can't. I remember. I remember who it was. My contact after Waterman left. The one who arranged for Milton One to come to me in my jail cell."

"Calm down. Calm down. I don't understand you."

"He was the one who whispered in my ear that I should find Waterman. He was the one who unlocked my handcuffs."

"You're not making any sense."

I looked at her tired, kind, and peaceful face. I could see her through the images of my dream that kept flashing before me. The dark maze. The white room. The blooming roses.

"I am making sense," I told her. "I finally remember. It was Rose. He's my contact. It was Detective Rose."

CHAPTER TWENTY-EIGHT
They're Here

Margaret helped me to a chair. I sank into it. I shivered, feeling cold wearing only my boxers and T-shirt. Sport sat beside me and sniffed at me with concern.

"Let me get your clothes," Margaret said.

She left me there. I hugged myself for warmth. The dog watched me eagerly. I looked up and saw Larry watching me eagerly too, staring at me over the back of the sofa with wide, worried eyes. I tried to wink and smile at him, to reassure him.

"It's all right," I said. "It's going to be all right."

He sank down a little behind the couch, but his eyes continued to peer at me over the top of it. The dog lay down at my feet.

A moment later Margaret came back carrying the rest of my clothing: the jeans, the sweatshirt, the fleece, the socks, all freshly washed and folded. I talked while I put the clothes on.

"I had a dream . . . ," I told her. "Only it was more than a dream. You know? It was like a memory only with symbols standing in for things, if you see what I'm saying."

"I see," said Margaret. "Go ahead."

"I was in this maze . . . I think that was supposed to represent my memory . . . and all along the walls of the maze, there were these vines with thorns on them. I didn't realize what they were at first, but then, in the dream, they blossomed and I saw they were rosebushes. And there was this guy at the center of the maze who talked to me, who helped me. He was my ally. Only I couldn't see his face. He was like the vines: I didn't know who he was. But when the vines blossomed . . ."

"No!" said Margaret. She understood a moment before I explained it.

"Yeah," I said, nodding slowly, remembering the blossoming walls of the maze. "They were rosebushes. And the guy in the maze was Rose. He was my ally. He was the one who told me about the device in my mouth, about how the Homelanders were going to break me out of prison. He was Waterman's contact on the police department. It was Rose all along."

"Are you sure, Charlie?" Margaret asked me. "He didn't seem like any kind of ally when he was just here."

I stood out of my chair to pull the sweatshirt down over my head. "I'm sure. I remember it now. It all makes sense. Just after I escaped from the Homelanders the first time, I was arrested. I was handcuffed and Rose and a bunch of deputies took me to a car to take me back to jail. But just before they put me in the car, someone unlocked my handcuffs and whispered in my ear, 'Find Waterman.' It was Rose. It must've been—he was the only one close enough to do it. I guess he couldn't help me more than that without giving himself away. Later, I saw my chance and I escaped—but he must've given me that chance, must've let me do it. Where are my shoes?"

"What do you need your shoes for? You're still sick. You're too weak to go anywhere now."

I looked at her for a moment, at her kind and tired face, her kind and tired eyes. I did my best to smile.

"I'll be fine," I told her. "Remember you talked about

doing what you have to do? Now I know what I have to do."

She hesitated another moment, then did her best to smile back. "I'll get your sneakers."

They were right there, against the wall by the computer table. She handed them to me. I sat down and put them on.

"What are you planning?" she asked me.

"I'm going to find him. Rose. He's the only contact I have left, the only one I can get to anyway. Maybe he can set things straight once and for all."

"Wait," said Margaret. She went back to the alcove, back to the table. She picked up a small rectangle of cardboard lying next to the laptop. She held it up. "You don't have to go anywhere," she said. "He gave me his card. He said I should call him if I saw you. We can just call him and he'll come. He'll know what to do."

She went to the phone.

"No," I said. "Let me. I don't want anyone to think you're calling for help. If the other police think you're in danger, one of them might shoot me or something. It would ruin my whole day."

She nodded. She picked up the phone's handset and gave it to me.

From the sofa, there came a short laugh. "'Ruin my whole day,'" Larry repeated, getting the joke. He was listening to every word we said.

I laughed. Suddenly, I was feeling pretty good, pretty hopeful. If I was right—if Rose was on my side—if I had at least one friend in the police department—the situation might not be as bad as I thought it was.

Margaret read the phone number aloud off the card. I keyed the numbers into the phone. I held the phone to my ear. It was silent.

"I guess I didn't do that right," I said. "Read me the number again."

She read the number again. This time, I pressed the Talk button first, then dialed the number. But when I held the phone to my ear, there was still nothing. It was still silent.

I pressed the Talk button. Listened. No dial tone.

"How do I get a dial tone?"

Margaret took the phone. Pressed the button. Listened. "Seems to be out. Maybe the battery . . ." She tapped the buttons, repeating Rose's phone number out loud a third time as she did. She listened. Shook her head.

"You have a cell?"

She left the room to get it. I heard her footsteps on

the kitchen linoleum. A moment later, she was back with her cell phone.

"The kitchen phone is dead too," she said.

The first tremor of fear went through me. I opened her cell. Looked at it. "No signal."

Margaret shook her head. "That's impossible. There's a cell tower just up the road. I always get full bars." She took the phone. Stared at it. Stared at me. "How is that possible?"

I didn't want her to see the fear in my eyes, but I knew she did. My voice was hoarse and tense as I said to her: "Get the boy out of here."

It took only a second for Margaret to understand. It was the Homelanders. It had to be. They had cut her phone lines, jammed her cell.

Now I could see the fear come into Margaret's eyes too. She gave a quick glance at her son, a quick shake of her head. When she spoke again, she dropped her voice low, hoping the boy wouldn't hear.

"They must already be here. Outside."

I turned to look at the window. Nothing visible out there but darkness; night. But I knew she had to be right. Why would they have cut the phones if they weren't here, ready to make their move?

The boy went on staring at us over the back of the couch. I sensed his worried eyes on me. I tried to look relaxed. But I dropped my voice to a whisper too.

"We probably don't have a lot of time."

"No time, more like," Margaret said.

"Is there a way out from upstairs?"

She thought for a second. Then she gestured at her son. "He's light enough to climb down the drainpipe. He's done it before."

"Wait till they're in the house," I said. "Then tell him to go into the woods and hide."

She was already moving to the sofa. She grabbed Larry's hand.

"Come on," she said.

"Where we going, Mommy?" Larry piped.

"Up to the attic."

He dragged his heels. "But I want to see the end of the movie."

Margaret gave his arm a good stiff tug. "Don't you argue with me, boy. Come on!"

"But Mommy . . . !"

"Hurry!"

With her other hand, she took Sport by the collar and pulled him along as well.

They all went up the stairs quickly.

My eyes went back to the front window. Out there in the dark, looking in at us here in the lighted house, they'd be able to see every move we made.

I went to the light switch. I turned the top light off, then moved around the room, killing whatever lights I found—including the TV still showing the DVD. There were still lights in the hall, some in the kitchen. I turned those off too. Now the house was almost as dark as the night outside.

I waited in that dark. Long minutes went by. I looked out the kitchen windows. I saw nothing. I listened. The house creaked and settled, but there was no other sound.

I began to wonder if maybe I'd been wrong. Maybe the Homelanders weren't here after all.

After a few more minutes, I felt my way through the dark house back into the living room. I took a step toward the front window, to see if I could get another angle on the outdoors, maybe spot something on the front drive.

Before I took a second step, the door burst open and the Homelanders came charging in.

CHAPTER TWENTY-NINE

Caught

There were three of them. They had machine guns with flashlights mounted on the barrels. The effect of the lights was awful, like something out of a horror movie. All I could see in the darkness of the house were the criss-crossing white beams, and the black death-dealing bores of the gun barrels, and the gunmen's twisted grimaces and hate-filled eyes half illuminated in the outglow of the light.

The deafening crash of the door bursting in stunned

me. The moving light beams dazzled me. But in the instant before they spotted my location, I managed to make my move.

I leapt away from the window and dove for the living room floor.

"There he is!" someone shouted.

There was a coughing burst of gunfire. A stuttering flash of flame. I heard glass breaking as bullets flew through the room. I heard Sport barking wildly somewhere far away. I hit the floor and rolled beneath the crisscrossing beams of light.

I rolled to my feet and ran in the direction of the dining room archway. The light beams scanned the darkness. I saw the archway—the dark shape of it in the half-lit shadows. Then the lights found me. I dove again as the gunfire exploded behind me. I felt a terrifying breath of air as a bullet whistled past my ear.

I hit the floor and somersaulted, rolling through the arch. I dodged to the side as the lights went back and forth through the darkness above me like the spotlights at some nightmare movie premiere. The beams flashed in a mirror on the dining room wall. The guns stuttered death and the mirror shattered, the light flying everywhere in a weirdly beautiful and sparkling chaos.

I got behind the wall and crouched low. I heard a Homelander bark a gruff command.

"Find the lights. I'll find *him*."

One flashlight beam broke off from the others and moved toward the dining room, where I was. The other two must've gone off looking for a light switch.

I crouched behind the wall, waiting. As long as the house lights were off, I had a small advantage: I could track them by their flashlights, but they couldn't track me.

Now, though, as I crouched, waiting, my heart hammering in my chest, a wave of weakness went over me. In the first moments of the Homelanders' invasion, a rush of adrenaline had given me new energy. But underneath that energy, I was still totally weak and exhausted from my illness and from the memory attacks. I didn't know if I had the strength to fight now. I knew I couldn't fight for long. Whatever I did, it was going to have to be quick.

The flashlight beam came toward the room, sweeping back and forth, trying to pick me out of the darkness. I crouched low behind the wall waiting.

The flashlight's advance halted.

"Turn the lights on, would you!" the gunman shouted with a curse. He didn't want to come through the archway until he could see. And yet, he started up again, kept coming forward cautiously toward the archway as I crouched there, waiting.

A voice shouted back, "I'm looking for the switch!"

The gunman stepped through the arch. Instantly, he swept the light toward me, searching me out, ready to gun me down. Because I was crouched so low, the light passed over my head. Still, the gunman spotted me in the outglow.

But by then, it was too late.

I hurled myself at him, coming in under the barrel of the gun. With all the strength I had left, I shouldered the gun barrel upward. At the same time, I struck at him low and hard. The gunman let out a gasp of pain and doubled over. His body went slack and started toppling down.

With my other hand, I grabbed the barrel of the gun. As he fell, already unconscious, I wrestled the weapon away from him, holding him up only long enough to pull the strap over his head.

Now I had the gun.

Just then, the lights went on.

There was only one Homelander in the living room. It was the fat guy with the stupid face who had been guarding the entrance to the compound. He was holding his machine gun leveled right at me, right at my head—and he was ready to fire and gun me down.

He had one problem. I was holding a machine gun too. And it was leveled at him. And my finger was also on the trigger.

"Drop it," the fat guy growled.

"You first," I growled back.

I moved into the living room, circling away from him, trying to get in a position where I could keep an eye on both him and the guard who had fallen unconscious in the dining room. The fat Homelander circled away from me too. We both kept our guns trained on each other.

Somewhere upstairs, I heard Sport barking and barking. He hadn't stopped since the Homelanders broke in.

"You think you can outshoot me?" the fat Homelander said to me. "I can kill you before you pull the trigger."

"Maybe," I answered him. "Or maybe you miss and die. Wanna take your chance?"

"*You're finished, West!*"

It was another voice, thick and guttural. Waylon's voice. I recognized it right away.

My eyes flicked to the sound of it, and what I saw made my blood turn to ice.

Waylon was just coming down the stairs. He had Margaret with him. He was holding her in front of him, with his arm around her throat. He had a 9mm pistol pressed to the side of her head.

"We've been watching the house, you know," Waylon said. "We saw her go upstairs with the boy. That idiot dog's barking led us right to her."

I could still hear Sport barking wildly, locked in a room upstairs, I guessed. And I thought: *The boy. Larry. What about Larry? Where was he?*

My eyes went to Margaret's eyes. I saw the terror in them as Waylon pressed the gun to her. But I saw something else too. She was trying to tell me something. She made an almost imperceptible gesture—a little shake of the head: the boy was gone. She'd gotten him out of the house. Down the drainpipe, into the woods. Just like I'd told her.

I kept my gun trained on the fat guard, but I spoke to Waylon through gritted teeth.

"Let her go," I said. "She has nothing to do with this."

"I'll let her go," Waylon answered. "Just as soon as you put the gun down. On the other hand, if you refuse, I'm going to blow her head off."

I hesitated, trying to think of something to do.

"Do you doubt that I'll do it?" Waylon said.

I didn't doubt it. I laid the machine gun on the floor.

"Now put your hands up."

The breath came out of me in a sigh of surrender. I put my hands up.

It was over. I was caught.

CHAPTER THIRTY

Out of the Darkness

For a moment, we stood frozen that way: Waylon with Margaret held to him, the gun at her head. The fat guard with his machine gun trained on me. The other guard, a tall, slender olive-skinned man, lying stationary on the living room floor. And me, with my hands in the air. We were all motionless and silent. Upstairs, the dog went on barking.

Then Waylon let Margaret go. He shoved her. She stumbled forward until she was standing next to me. He pointed his pistol in our direction.

"Should I kill them?" said the fat guard.

I glanced at him, off to my left. I could see in his eyes that he was eager to pull the trigger.

Waylon thought about it. Behind his scruffy black beard, his heavy features worked slowly.

"No," he said quietly. "Not yet. I still want to find out what he knows." Then, after a pause, he added very casually, "But the woman—she is useless to me. Kill her."

The fat gunman didn't hesitate to do as he was ordered. The barrel of his machine gun swung from me to Margaret. I saw the gunman's finger begin to tighten on the trigger.

I grabbed Margaret by the arm and pulled her behind me. I stood between her and the gun.

The fat gunman let out a curse. "Get out of the way, punk!"

I stood motionless and answered him with an empty stare. He couldn't kill Margaret without shooting me, so for a moment—a second, two, three—he was paralyzed. But it was really we—Margaret and I—who were out of options, out of hope. I could delay the inevitable for only a little while, but the chase, in fact, was finished. I knew we were both less than a minute away from death.

"I'm sorry I brought this on you," I said to Margaret over my shoulder.

"No, it's on all of us," she answered back. "It always has been."

Waylon laughed, his white teeth flashing. "Very touching. Very heroic. Very moving." He shook his head, still grinning. "All right, West," he said to me. "You win. You win at last. I had orders to question you, but you've made it impossible. Congratulations, tough guy." Turning to the fat gunman, he said, "I've had enough of this. Kill them both."

"Drop it!"

Everyone in the room froze. The command had come from the open door of the house. I turned and saw nothing there—nothing but the night and darkness.

Then out of the darkness stepped Detective Rose, a pistol in his hand. He held the gun high in both hands and kept it trained on the fat gunman.

"Put the gun down right now," he said.

The fat gunman hesitated and Rose fired off a round. He lifted the barrel of his pistol so that the bullet flew over the fat gunman's head. It crashed into the wall, opening a small black hole and sending a puff of plaster into the room.

That was all the fat gunman needed to see. Terrified, he immediately stripped his machine-gun strap over his head and dropped the weapon to the floor. He put his hands up.

But not Waylon.

While Rose's attention was on the fat gunman, Waylon turned and leveled his 9mm at the detective. I saw it— but I was too far away to do anything about it.

My arms flew out helplessly. I shouted, "Rose, watch out!"

Rose turned and Waylon fired at him and Rose fired back all in the same instant.

The room seemed to quake with the deafening explosions. My eyes wide, I saw the frame of the door go jagged as splinters flew out of it. Waylon had missed.

For what seemed like a long, long second, the two men just stood there with their guns trained on each other. It was weirdly quiet. It came to me that Sport had stopped barking upstairs, as if he were listening too, waiting to find out what had happened.

Then Waylon looked down in surprise to see the black hole that had appeared in his chest.

The next moment, the terrorist collapsed to the floor, dead.

CHAPTER THIRTY-ONE

Don't Ever Be Afraid

Detective Rose stepped into the house—and now law enforcement officers came pouring in behind him. It seemed there was a whole army of them: state troopers in khaki, local cops in blue, detectives in jackets and ties. They filled the living room. Some of them grabbed hold of the fat guard. They threw his large body against the wall roughly. They wrestled his hands behind his back and snapped handcuffs on him. Others grabbed hold of the guard lying on the floor. He was starting to moan and shift around there. His eyes fluttered open and he let out a groan. By then a pair of troopers had him under the arms and were hauling him to his feet. They put his hands behind his back and handcuffed him too.

"This one's dead," said another trooper, kneeling over Waylon.

Rose nodded, holstering his gun. "We're all gonna miss him," he said drily. "He brought the world so much joy."

"Detective," said Margaret. The words seemed to break out of her: "My son. I sent him out to hide in the woods. He must be out there somewhere. He must be so afraid. Please find my son."

"We've already got him," said Rose.

"I'm here! I'm here, Mommy!"

A patrolman in a blue uniform came to the door holding Larry by the hand. The child broke away from him and ran into the room. He ran to Margaret and threw his arms around her.

Margaret hugged him, closing her eyes, tears pouring down her cheeks. It was a long hug, but finally, Margaret kneeled down so that she was at eye level with her son. She held him by the shoulders.

"Are you all right?" she said, crying. "Are you hurt? Where were you?"

"I didn't go into the woods, Mommy," Larry said in his piping voice. "I know you said to, but I didn't want to leave you alone. I ran down the street to Mrs. Carter's house. I used her phone and called the number."

Margaret shook her head, confused. "What number?"

"The number you kept saying. The one on the card. You and Charlie were trying to call it, but the phone was broken. You kept saying the number, so I remembered it and I called it and told Detective Rose we were in trouble and he came."

"We had a search headquarters set up just down the road," said Rose. "We were less than two minutes away."

Margaret wrapped her arms around Larry and started to sob helplessly.

"Second floor's clear," said a cop on the stairs—and as he spoke, Sport, released from wherever he'd been locked up, came bounding down to us. He joined Larry and Margaret and danced around them, panting happily.

"What about this one?" said a trooper. He was standing next to me. He put his hand on my arm.

Rose looked at me. His flat face was expressionless. His sharp eyes were distant and cold.

"Cuff him," he said. "He's a fugitive wanted for murder. I'm here to take him back to prison."

The trooper grabbed me by the arm and the shoulder. "Hands behind your back," he ordered.

I put my hands behind my back. I kept looking at Rose. Rose kept looking at me, his eyes cold. But still, somehow, I thought I saw something in them. Some recognition. Some message of encouragement. I hoped I saw that anyway. I hoped I was right about him and that he really was my ally.

The trooper put handcuffs on my wrists.

Sport barked a protest at them.

"Why are they arresting Charlie?" Larry cried out in distress.

I smiled down at him. "It's all right, Larry," I said. "It's going to be all right."

"But they're arresting him, Mommy! Why are they arresting him?"

"Ssh," she said.

"Don't worry, Larry," I told him, trying to smile. "Don't be afraid. It's going to be all right, you hear me? Don't ever be afraid."

The trooper grabbed me by the shoulder again. He started pressing me toward the door.

I held back. I turned to Margaret. "Thank you," I said. "God bless you."

She shook her head. "God bless you," she said. "Don't you be afraid either."

"I'm not afraid," I told her. "I'm not afraid."

The trooper turned to Rose. Rose kept looking at me.

"Charlie West," Rose said, "you're under arrest for murder and escape." Then he added to the trooper, "Take him in."

The trooper marched me out the door and into the darkness.

Reading Group Guide

1. As the title of this part of Charlie's story indicates, the answers about the past year are slowly starting to come. What part of the truth was most surprising to you?

2. Charlie says "I knew it wasn't about things being fair. It wasn't about them being easy or safe. It was about who I was, who I wanted to be, what I wanted my life to be about, what I wanted to stand for, live for, even die for it I had to. It was about what I wanted to make out of this soul God gave me." Have you given much thought to what you want to make out of the soul God gave you? What are you willing to stand for? Are there any things you *wish* you were willing to stand for?

3. When Charlie eats the food from Margaret's refrigerator he leaves money in the lunch meat container to pay for it. Would you think to do that if you were

in Charlie's situation and running for your life? What do you think this action says about Charlie's character? Does it enforce character traits you've already seen in him or is does it show a new side?

4. Charlie ends up being protected by Margaret and Larry. If you came home and found a strange person there, what would you do? Why do you think that Margaret didn't immediately call the police?

5. Charlie describes Margaret as a woman who "looked and sounded like a woman who was on a long, hard journey but knew she was headed for a good place." Do you know anyone you would describe that way? What good place do you think Margaret is headed for?

6. Were you surprised by Charlie's dream about roses? What do you think is going to happen now that Rose has arrested him?

An Interview with
Andrew Klavan

Q: There's one book left in Charlie's story—*The Final Hour*, available August 2011. Any hint as to what's going to happen to him?

ANDREW KLAVAN: Well, if you've come to the end of *The Truth of the Matter*, you should have a pretty good sense of, you know, the truth of the matter: who Charlie is and how he got into this situation. But there are still some pieces of the puzzle missing. And, as so often happens in life, the final pieces can change the whole picture. I will say this: *The Final Hour* is also Charlie's darkest hour—a real nightmare of a situation where he and some of the people he loves are put in positions where they have to risk the ultimate sacrifice. So the story is close to ending—but it's far from over!

Q: Why did you choose to make karate such a big part of Charlie's life?

AK: Partly it was personal: my own enjoyment of the sport, my own feeling that it's cool to do and my own pride in having earned a black belt. Partly, I thought it was good storytelling: if I was going to throw Charlie into a desperate situation, I wanted him to have some resources of physical and mental skill—I didn't want him simply to be running away and hiding all the time. But also, and maybe this is the most important reason, there are certain values inherent in martial arts training that I think we talk about way too little and that I think are central to living at a high level. Paying attention, joyful self-discipline, focus. I wanted Charlie at his best to be able to exemplify that way of life.

Q: What aspect of Charlie's character do you most hope readers will remember?

AK: His fortitude . . . Ha, there's an old-fashioned word for you. It means: "mental and emotional strength in facing difficulty, adversity, danger, or temptation courageously." See, a person can have courage in battle but fold his cards the minute things get tough emotionally. Or he can speak his beliefs boldly, but then turn into a mouse the minute he faces a physical threat. But someone with fortitude never gives in. Charlie has moments of real terror and even one or two moments of actual despair. But he always finds a way to fight out of it. He never gives in. Most of us aren't going to be wanted for murder and chased by terrorists, but we are going to face grief and sickness, loss and the failure of hope, times when the best we can do is bear down and keep on, keep heading toward the light. I want people to remember how Charlie keeps on.

Q: What's the most interesting question you've been asked by a fan of this series? How did you respond?

AK: Well, I get asked a lot of questions about Charlie's patriotism and I always find that interesting—even peculiar in a way. There's a school of thought today that rejects patriotism. People are made nervous by that intense allegiance to country. They think it can only lead to war and bloodshed and that fights can be avoided if we all just compromise and get along. And, of course, compromise and getting along are great things as long as you're not sacrificing essential values. But I believe there's a line in the sand, some things that you have to be willing to stand up for, even if it means trouble. Charlie's patriotism is not blind, flag-waving jingoism: it's an intense allegiance to the American concept of liberty. He's thought it through. He can talk about it and explain it. And he's shown he's willing to give everything for it. I admire him for that.

Q: The Homelanders Series has been optioned for film. Who optioned it? Any idea when we might see Charlie on the big screen?

AK: Yeah, I'm excited about that. The series was optioned by Summit Entertainment. They're the people who make the *Twilight* movies. The last news I got, they were looking for someone to write the script and they believed they were close to hiring someone. I've had a few books made into movies and my experience is that things move very slowly—and then very fast. They go along trying to put things together, working on the script, going down dead ends and you think, "Well, this'll never happen"— and then suddenly they start filming and the picture is done. So you basically just have to stay both hopeful and patient.

Q: Do you have plans to write any more young adult novels once the Homelanders Series is complete?

AK: Absolutely. I've loved writing Charlie, and I'll be sorry when the Homelanders saga is complete and I have to say goodbye to him, but at the same time, I really enjoy doing new things and starting on something original. Plus I've got lots of other great stories I'm dying to tell. My plan now is to write some singleton novels—non-series stories that begin and end in a single book. I've already got the first one all worked out in my head— my publisher, Thomas Nelson, and I have made all the arrangements—so yeah, I'm ready to go!

THE FINAL HOUR

THE
HOMELANDERS

———

BOOK FOUR

**AVAILABLE
AUGUST 2011**

About the Author

 **Andrew Klavan** was hailed by Stephen King as "the most original novelist of crime and suspense since Cornell Woolrich." He is the recipient of two Edgar Awards and the author of such bestsellers as *True Crime* and *Don't Say a Word.*